FEMINIZED AND PRETTY

1

Force-feminized by his vengeful wife (Femdom and Transgender)

Lady Alexa

Copyright © Lady Alexa 2021

All rights reserved. No reproduction, copy or transmission of this publication or section in this publication may be reproduced copied or transmitted without written permission of the author.

This novel is a work of fiction. Names, characters, businesses, places, events and incidents are either the products of the author's imagination or used in a fictitious manner. Any resemblance to actual persons, living or dead, or actual events is purely coincidental.

Contains explicit scenes of a sexual nature including male to female gender transformation, female domination, CFNM, spanking and reluctant feminisation. All characters in this story are aged 18 and over.

Strictly for adults aged 18 and over.

Dear Reader,

I hope you enjoy the first of the three-part series: 'Feminized and Pretty'.

Why not subscribe to my blog at www.ladyalexauk.com where I write about my true-life FLR lifestyle with my feminised husband, Alice, the source of many of my ideas for my novels. I cover the advantages of this lifestyle as well as some of the challenges.

You can also subscribe to my newsletter from the sidebar form and receive free and exclusive forced-feminisation and femdom stories, additional chapters from my books and serialised stories through the newsletter, also available on the blog and special offers

CONTENTS

Chapter 1 — I'm going to feminise him

Chapter 2 — A new submissive life

Chapter 3 — The plan goes awry

Chapter 4 — Homecoming queen

Chapter 5 — The marriage contract

Chapter 6 — His wife's the boss

Chapter 7 — The office junior

Chapter 8 — The new junior admin girl

Chapter 9 — A pretty skirt

Chapter 10 — A short skirt and hairy legs

Chapter 11 — Vulnerable

Chapter 12 — Covering his little dignity

Chapter 13 — Smooth & feminine

Chapter 14 — Escape plans

Chapter 15 — Kitchen humiliation

Chapter 16 — Makeup time

Chapter 17 — Runaway

Chapter 18 — Refuge

Chapter 19 — Auntie's home

Chapter 20 — Surprise surprise

Chapter 1 — I'm going to feminise him

"I'm going to humiliate, punish and feminise him."

She listened with shock at what her older sister, Elizabeth, had said to her. It was harsh and vindictive but she did understand the problem her sister had with her husband. She respected her sister's opinion. Nonetheless, it seemed strange to her: humiliation and feminisation? Punish?

Elizabeth always called her 'Sis'. They were half-sisters but the bond was strong. Sis had a pet name for her older sibling too: Red. That was on account of her infamous temper. A temper that was never directed at her; it was regularly pointed at employees, suppliers, her boyfriends and now her husband. Any male.

Sis had heard her say similar things about humiliating and even feminising men before; she was never sure if she was joking. She knew all about Red's new husband and how Red had developed that relationship. Red had wanted someone young, attractive and pliable. Someone to own and control.

Her sister was like that.

But Red had made a mistake this time and her supposedly pliable husband had tried to be manipulative himself. Red's vengeance would be swift and complete.

Sis looked down at the wooden floor of the bar as if the boards would help her find the right words. "I know you chose him carefully so you could control him but tell me you're joking. You're not going to make him live as a girl, are you? You're going to do that to him? Isn't it a bit extreme? Put him in dresses and skirts? Isn't that weird? Humiliate him? And what does cuckold mean? You said earlier you want to cuckold him as that excites you?"

Red didn't blink; she crossed her long elegant legs. A twitch in her eye and the corner of her mouth. Sis knew she was in a privileged position; she was the only one Red allowed to challenge her. Her older sister always tolerated her, it was a baby sister's privilege.

"So many questions, Sis." She smiled. "I'm going to make him feel vulnerable, humiliated and subjugated. I will control everything about him. My original plan was to find a weak man I could mould to how I wanted him to be, like a piece of pliable clay. I do like a nice submissive feminised man to own and design, a blank canvas to play with. It's more fun when they resist. Now I want vengeance too. How dare he try to do what he did."

"But he failed," Sis pointed out.

"It doesn't matter. My original plan to make him a pliable feminised male remains, plus a whole lot more for my no-good husband. It was the intention of what he planned to do that mattered. And the thought he could outsmart me. Besides, I wanted to go the whole way anyhow; now I have an excuse. It's exciting that I can turn him into a girl. A girl I can design myself. A submissive girl. That's real power, Sis." She beamed at the prospect.

They were sharing a glass of wine, it was early evening on a gloomy Saturday. They were seated in the bay window of a trendy and expensive wine bar just outside the north-east corner of Central London. The air inside the bar tasted of fresh coffee, wine and sweet spices. Bland piped jazz music hummed in the background from hidden speakers. The rough nailed pine floor and red-brick walls gave the bar the appearance of an ancient Victorian drinking establishment. It had been built in 2015. The tourists and other visitors were impressed; the locals were indifferent.

The first spots of rain hit the bar's double-glazed plastic imitation sash windows' like tiny grains of rice thrown at a wedding. Grey September clouds covered the sky, threatening a downpour. A sickly orange glow, from a street lamp in the alley outside, shone into their white wine glasses. At the end of the alley, the headlight beams of the evening traffic shone gloomily; the high road was clogged in the gloomy autumn evening.

Sis looked into Red's cool brown eyes, they were like large frozen almonds. Red's success had come from a keen intellect and an inability to tolerate mediocrity. It also came from long hard work for long late hours. Sis knew Red was always in her office by 7 am sharp every morning and worked until late in the evening.

"Men are selfish. It's always about them and their needs. I should have known, Sis. There's little else going on in their little minds. You'll learn Sis, I did."

Sis looked down at the floorboards again. There was a large age difference between them: twenty-five years. They were the products of two different marriages and a mother restarting late in life after an abusive first husband; Red's estranged father. Their mother had found happiness the second time with a younger kinder man, Sis's father.

They had no worries about their mother now. He looked after her. They joked he was like a housewife to their mother. He fussed around her and always served teas and biscuits when they visited. And that apron, too frilly and flowery to be masculine. Never mind, he was kind to her. His hair was far too long and blonde for a fifty-five-year-old man. But as long as their mother was happy, who cared?

Sis had just finished university, twenty-three and innocent. She looked up to her older sister Red. Sis saw confidence, assertiveness and power. Red was the founder and owner of a product design company in Shoreditch, east London, where they were now sitting. What had once been a gritty inner-city borough, was now a hub of technology and design studios.

Red's company was one of the largest and most well-known in the UK. It was the end of Sis's first week there. Red had given her a position as her Executive Assistant. It was a way to train her in business and it effectively made her the company's second-in-command. She loved being with Red and had jumped at her offer.

Red looked back into her sister's eyes and furrowed her forehead. "Oh, oh," thought Sis, "This is Red's serious face."

"Sis. You have everything you to succeed in our business."

She shuddered with pleasure at those words; *our business*. A catch came on her throat and she thought she might cry. Red saw her eyes water.

"Don't get upset." Red reached over across the small round table and stroked her sister's head. "But you need to toughen up. You're *too* nice. You have too much of your father in you." Red smiled and pulled her hand away from her sister's head. "Not all men are nice like your father, who I think of as my father too these days. Some men you have to train and some, like our father, are easier to train. In the end, they all submit. They are naturally submissive, but it's often hidden beneath layers of false bravado and artificial masculinity. Masculinity is a false state, a fake way of living. There is only femininity and it's our role to uncover it in the males in our lives and to help it flourish. We are their guides, even if they don't know it. If you don't control them and feminise them, then you have what I found in my father and my new husband. Deceit. I should have acted more quickly. It was a learning process for me too. Now I have to punish him. It would have been so unnecessary if I had only feminised him properly from the start of our relationship."

A silence fell over the pair, invisible connections flowed between the two sisters. It wasn't always necessary to speak to understand — the tutor and the pupil.

Sis spotted Red's face change. She looked across at two middle-aged men at the table next to them. They sipped at amber-coloured craft beers, *Made in Camden* etched on the bulbous glasses. Their dark-blue suit jackets were pulled tight by their large stomachs; it looked like they had cushions shoved inside their shirts. The buttons creaked and the seams were stretched taut over the flab. They had spent too many evenings drinking beer and eating takeaway food. They stared as they listened to what Red was saying. Red stared back.

A moment passed by and one winked at Red. "Hello, darling. Do you want to join us? You need a real man from what I was listening to."

Red's face went puce, proving her nickname to be accurate. "See what I mean, Sis? Those two need to be put in maid's dresses and made to clean for us. And then spanked to show respect." Red put out a manicured finger pointing at the men, the long nail was like a lioness's claw about to strike them.

Sis cringed at the volume at which Red had spoken and the way she now pointed. People looked. Red stared back at the overweight businessmen and shook her head. She threw back her dark-brown mane of long waving hair. Diamond-encrusted drop earrings caught the sodium street lighting and flashed at the businessmen like a warning signal. Red put her hands back on the square wooden tabletop on either side of her wine glass. Her flame-red long nail tips on the surface. The men stared, leering happily. They still thought they were funny.

"So you want to come back to my house and clean for me?

Good. After I've put you in pretty dresses, I'll spank your fat arses with a riding crop before clamping cages on your pathetic little cocks. You'll then kiss my feet." She leant forward. "Shall we go, sissies?" The room went silent as her words echoed off the exposed brick walls.

The two men drained their glasses and their eyes flicked back and forth to each other, assessing the situation. It had changed rapidly. Their faces flushed as the customers watched the unfolding event with interest. A squealed female's stifled laugh pealed out from the other side of the bar. One of the businessmen mumbled something and they got up, scraping their chairs back along the floor like chalk on a blackboard. The sisters watched as the men bundled out of the door, crashing together in their haste. They squeezed out and into the spitting rain.

Sis giggled. "Red, you are terrible." They touched each other's arms affectionately.

"I have a lot to teach you about how to treat males, little Sis. Follow my lead and you'll learn well. We'll be starting your lessons tomorrow with my *dear* husband."

Chapter 2 — A new submissive life

Three weeks before the meeting with Sis in the wine bar, Elizabeth dozed gently beside her new husband, Patrick. Her feet were up in the wide first-class aeroplane seat and with the back flat back. Elizabeth was tall, slim and elegant even in sleep. Even after eight hours in flight, there was not a crease on her skirt nor a hair out of place. Her long brown hair was deliberately tussled in the same manicured style as when they had boarded the aeroplane.

Some people slept with their mouths open, occasionally snoring or snorting. Not Elizabeth. Even in sleep, she had the elegance and bearing of a queen. After their six-month whirlwind courtship, he still couldn't believe his luck. An expensive marriage to a beautiful millionaire and then a luxurious honeymoon. They were now on their way home to start married life.

He watched her sleeping. Elizabeth may have been nearly twenty years older than him but she was still fantastic looking. He was 28 and a good-looking slim man, he knew that. He confirmed it to himself regularly in any mirror he came across. His long dark hair was swept back from his face. Elizabeth had encouraged him to grow it long from the moment they had met, six months ago. She said it suited him better for what she had in mind. He wasn't sure what she meant by that but she was odd.

He didn't spend too much effort thinking about the odd things she said or did. If she wanted his hair long, he'd grow it long. It made him even more interesting, he guessed. It also suited his profession as a musician; it wasn't out of place. What was out of place was that Elizabeth had recently started to take him with her to her hair salon. It was embarrassing but she told him it was a unisex place. He had never seen any other men there but why would she lie?

The last time they had been there, the hairdresser had styled his hair under the supervision of Elizabeth. It was a little feminine. *Nonsense,* Elizabeth had said when he mentioned it. The stylist had given him a fringe and curled the ends under in a bob effect. He hated it and brushed it back later using gel. It was the look he wore now. She'd styled it herself in the hotel room every morning of their honeymoon and before they'd left for the airport.

He inspected his nails. Hey were too long and perfectly shaped for his liking but Elizabeth preferred them that way. She took him to the nail bar after going to the hairdresser's. The light sheen on the nails was disconcerting. Elizabeth had said no one would ever notice transparent varnish with a light sheen.

On their last visit to the nail bar, she suggested an ivory shade. He hated going there and sitting with his hands on the desk while a young lady worked on his nails. The women on either side of him would stare. It did no harm, he supposed, and he liked being careful with his looks. He cringed when the beautician did his nails and Elizabeth stood over him giving instructions as his nails were done. The last two times Elizabeth had asked the lady doing his nails to put the transparent shellac on them. *To look after them*, she had said. He hadn't been consulted.

Recently, Elizabeth had started to prefer him not to wear any clothes at home. It was fun and sexy, she said. Nothing on.

Naked. She always remained dressed though. She had carried this odd practice through to the honeymoon. At first, he assumed she loved seeing his young fit body. It was probably a treat for her old eyes.

He asked her to be naked too, now that would have been fun. Elizabeth said it didn't work like that. Like what? He never found out. His belief it was a treat for her eyes had begun to founder a little. She sometimes seemed not to notice him as she did other things. Yet whenever he said he wanted to get dressed she said no. He had to remain naked. It was nice this way, she said.

If that was her way and if it was a turn-on for her, then so be it. He had a slim body so why not let his wife ogle it? It was embarrassing when she worked at home and asked him to bring her things and run around for her like he was a naked servant and her the mistress of the house. She told him not to be a silly boy. He put up with it. Her wealth was the focus, not her strange ways.

One day, he found his underwear drawer cleaned out and replaced with delicate female panties. She said she hated male underwear, it was unattractive. She said she would like him to wear the panties. It wasn't a request even though she had said it nicely enough. Panties felt nice enough and since she had thrown his male undies away, he had little choice. If she hadn't been rich, it may have been the end of the relationship. But she was rich and he wasn't. In the end, he shrugged and wore them. What harm did it do?

She constantly mentioned his body hair. He wasn't that hairy. Elizabeth said she didn't like body hair. She had suggested he remove it. She offered to pay for someone to wax him. She said it was very sexy. He'd refused. She was disappointed but hadn't pushed it.

He was not muscled or tall. He had a wiry slim figure like a long-distance runner. Elizabeth was an inch taller than him in bare feet and even taller in her heels. He had never had any problem meeting and bedding women; he always took care of his appearance. He had never dated a woman as old as his wife before but her looks and, more importantly, her wealth was more than a great compensation. And the key to his future wealth.

He was a singer and guitar player, it was how they had met. He had got a gig at an expensive wine bar in West London. It had been one of his better-paid jobs. Mostly he scraped by playing in rough pubs in between the performances from strippers and comedians. He spent his days working out in a council-run gym.

Elizabeth had gone to the wine bar with two other ladies. She had zeroed in on him like a guided missile during his break. The conversation had seemed like an interview, did he have a girlfriend? Friends, job? And so it went gone on. At the end of the night, she had said he seemed perfect material. They started to date and before long, the odd requests began.

He'd put up with it as he had to look for a change. His music career was going nowhere, that was obvious. He needed a way to get some money. Quickly and easily. Her money is what she wanted. And to become a Vice President at her company, that was what he expected. Why not, he was now her husband.

He used to live in a one-bed council apartment in a rough area of the city. He was out of her league on social and career levels. Elizabeth was a multi-millionaire business owner with a six-bed five-million-pound house with a basement swimming pool and a home cinema in the priciest areas.

She could have had anyone: a film star, another business owner or a premier-league footballer. But she had chosen him: a failing musician. He never asked himself why she had chosen him, he assumed it was because he was attractive and desirable. It was natural, wasn't it? He had to admit, he was a smooth operator.

It had been his first time flying first class and he had overdone the free champagne again. It had been the same story on their honeymoon in the Maldives on an exclusive holiday island hideaway. The only other guests on the island were a couple of American high-tech company owners with their partners and a middle-aged Russian businessman with a bleach-blond eighteen-year-old 'wife' and his two unfriendly military-looking bodyguards.

The captain announced they had thirty minutes to landing. Home. He glanced across to his sleeping wife again and out of the portal window. A sea of red-tiled semi-detached house roofs were broken up by waves of retail areas filled with rectangular warehouses. The ocean of civilisation was split in half by the snaking grey thread of the wide lazy river. The roads below bristled with red stop lights, back to back in the caterpillar-like grid-locked traffic. The plane banked and the concrete strips of the airport lined up ahead.

A stewardess leant across. He gave her his toothy grin, the one that always worked with the women. She ignored him and touched the top of Elizabeth's slim hand who woke instantly without looking as if she had even been asleep.

"Madam, we'll be landing shortly. Please bring your seat up, put your footrest down and fasten your seat belt." A faint practised smile came from the stewardess.

"Of course," Elizabeth said as if she had never been asleep.

"Hello, Liz, did you have a nice doze?" He smiled at her. She glared back her face stern.

"Sorry, I mean Elizabeth." He swallowed hard. She hated her name being abbreviated.

"Better," she replied not bothering to answer his original question.

Chapter 3 — The plan goes awry

He had certainly won the lottery of life when he married this stunning wealthy lady. He guessed her unusual behaviour came with the territory. She hated having her name shortened by anyone and that included him. After six months together, he usually remembered. The long flight had made him tired and he had forgotten.

He didn't mind her calling him Pat instead of Patrick, even though it was one rule for her and another for him. He had to put up with her ways; she was the boss in their relationship. He went with that but now things would change. Now he had her. He inspected his gold wedding band. The control would surely change now he had her legally.

He watched her from the corner of his eye as he felt his ears block up from the change in pressure. The plane descended towards the airport. He knew not to make small talk, she hated it.

They would be met at the airport by her driver. This was a new world for him. The luxury and the lifestyle. He felt like a boy locked in a sweet shop and told to take anything he wanted. He now had a sexy, beautiful, wealthy older wife, almost old enough to be his mother. If he could have designed a wife by looks, she would look like Elizabeth but younger. The single worry buzzing in his head was her recent poor attitude towards him — cold and detached.

They were going to live at her massive home. She had insisted they live apart before the honeymoon but now they were married he was going straight back to her place to set up home together. As man and wife. He smirked at the thought. Who would have guessed that he, Patrick Ashleigh, would have got married so young? Who would have thought he would have got married at all?

Elizabeth worked long hours but he imagined the late evenings and weekends having sex with his incredible wife. And when she was away working, then who knows what opportunities he would find? Her executive assistant, Charlotte, was cute and much younger. Elizabeth's personal assistant, Clara, was pretty hot too. He looked across at his wife again and felt a stirring. He hoped he wasn't too tired or hungover when they got back.

On reflection, he had probably overindulged while on the honeymoon. Maybe that was her problem. The champagne had been excellent and all-inclusive. Well, why not indulge? She had paid for it as part of the holiday cost, it would have been rude not to take advantage. He wasn't going to get married to a millionaire every day. It would have been a shame to waste it.

The first couple of days they had sex in their room. On her terms, of course, but that was fine. Elizabeth was a looker. Old, but sexy anyway. After that, he usually fell asleep after a bottle or two of the finest bubbly and a couple of brandies to finish the night off. There would be plenty of time for more sex when they got home.

Elizabeth had become annoyed with him after the first days. She was moody but he was certain all would be fine once they got home. All women were like that but they got over it eventually. She would too. She may be a CEO but underneath all the glamour and money, she was just a woman.

He heard his wife breathe in. That usually meant she was

about to speak. He waited, knowing not to interrupt first.

"Pat. Tomorrow is Saturday and you have lots to do. Tell me what you have to do?"

Pat looked around hoping no one heard her. She spoke to him as if he were a child. Or an idiot, setting him little tasks. She was still cold with him. What had got into her? She'd get over it, she couldn't keep up her moodiness forever although she'd been annoyed for over a week. She lasted longer than most women.

He had phoned his school friend Mike from the suite after Elizabeth had fallen asleep A couple of days into the honeymoon. He had wanted to complain. In his drunken ramblings, he had confided he didn't love Elizabeth, just her wealth. He conceded she was stunning to look at, even at her age. It wasn't hard to play-act as the loving partner. Maybe he shouldn't have told Mike but he would never say anything. No harm done.

He had told Mike that, after a couple of years, he planned to divorce Elizabeth and come away with part of her fortune and her company; a great investment for two years of his life.

He could buy a new guitar and have the money to go for a successful music career. His career had been held back by a lack of money and a poor guitar, that was all. Now things would be different. She had been asleep and Mike would keep his mouth shut: no harm done.

Elizabeth poked him. "Stop daydreaming."

He shook thoughts of the future divorce from his mind.

She wanted him to recite his tasks so she could check. He swallowed his pride. Think of two years' time and the divorce settlement, he told himself. Then a glittering music career with the proceeds of the settlement.

He recited back her instructions. "Move the last of my belongings to your place."

"Good boy and what else?" She looked at him through her long dark curled lashes. He went rigid at her comment, *good boy*. She often used that term. Whenever he objected, she asked if he would prefer she called him 'good girl'. She was odd.

He had to get used to her moods for the next two years so he batted his irritation away. It was worth it for the benefits their marriage would bring. "I will report to your office for my first day at your company tomorrow."

"At what time?"

"9 am, dear."

"Don't call me, *dear*, you know I don't like that."

"Yes, Elizabeth, I'm sorry," he said, remembering to use her full name.

"That's better. Good boy. I can see your training is going to be difficult. You've been good so far but the next phase will be a big change for you."

"Eh?" He asked. "Training? Next phase? What are you talking about?"

She didn't reply. Instead, she stretched to look out of the window. Ignoring him again. He had been concerned at her insistence he leave his job as a musician to work for her. It wasn't going well financially but it was fun and a great way to meet women. They all liked a musician, didn't they? Even Elizabeth. His idea had been to work for her and to continue evenings playing guitar and singing in pubs. She had told him what she wanted when she had proposed to him. Proposal was a strong word, it was an instruction to get married.

Giving up being a musician was a red line for her for reasons he didn't fully understand. But it was only temporary and it was worth the temporary suspension to ensnare her. After a couple of years, he would return to music. Anyway, it was obvious in the meantime she would give him a senior position in her company as he was her husband. It stands to reason. That wouldn't harm when the divorce happened. In two years.

Their plane wavered a few times and the wheels touched the runway. How jealous his friends were when they had seen her for the first time at their wedding. They had looked at her open-mouthed. He hadn't seen them much after he had met Elizabeth. She had told him he was too busy to see the now.

He remembered the discussion with her about him having to stop playing in pubs and bars. He had told her how he enjoyed his work and how he would one day possibly get a recording contract. She said it made more sense for him to work for her and have a steady job. In working for her they would be putting their combined energies into making wealth for themselves. He felt a vague discomfort he would be working for his wife.

He had also been a little discomforted about her vague answers to his assertion he would have a senior role. As her husband, why shouldn't he be a Vice President in her company? *Why not indeed* was her reply? He had tried to pin her down to what position she was going to give him. She had brushed him away by saying one that would suit his specific skills and experience and he was not to worry. He demanded the title of Vice President. She told him he could call himself whatever he wanted.

He had been happy at that. Vice President, he thought as he settled back while the plane taxied to the terminal. He felt a warm feeling of achievement. This was going to plan. He tried to push a nagging worry from the back of his mind. Elizabeth was always clear and focused. Why couldn't she be clear about his exact role in her company now? And why was she moody and curt with him?

Chapter 4 — Homecoming queen

Their long white Mercedes pulled up in front of the high metal gates. After a few moments, they opened inwards. Patrick felt a zing of intense excitement at his future as the opulence of the house now opened up for him behind the automatic gates.

The thoughts of work roles faded away. All was going to be fine. He would soon be a Vice President and rich. More than fine. Elizabeth looked straight ahead, impassive and controlled. It was as if he was looking at her through a wall of ice. When was her bad mood going to dissipate? She hadn't seemed the type but she could keep up a mood for days, that was sure. Typical. Once a woman had you trapped in a relationship, they changed and they tried to change you. To be honest, she had changed him a little already he reminded himself. Despite being a businesswoman, Elizabeth was still a woman underneath and operated like any other woman.

The driver steered the car into the driveway, gravel crunched under the tyres. They stopped in front of a large front door. Three wide red steps led up to a double-sized white front door. The young blond female driver jumped out with an energy that surprised Patrick. She opened Elizabeth's car door with a broad toothy smile.

"Thank you, Angie," Elizabeth said in a kind husky voice, a voice that had been missing for the past week.

Elizabeth pushed a long smooth leg out of the car. Patrick waited for Angie to come round to his side and to open his door. He felt as if he were in a kind of high-society aristocracy. A warm tingle flowed through his body. He had done well finding and hooking Elizabeth. To be honest, she found him, snaring him like a guided missile. He hadn't put up a fight once he found out how much she was worth.

Angie popped open the boot of the car. Elizabeth bent down and put her head through the open car door. "What are you waiting for?" She remained there looking agitated, one hand on the roof the other on a hip.

Patrick felt stupid. Angie was lifting their suitcases out of the rear of the car. She wasn't going to open his door. "Sorry dear, I mean Elizabeth. I was thinking how happy I was to be married to you."

Elizabeth breathed out sharply. "Well, why don't you think about getting out of the car and helping Angie with the luggage?"

She marched off, her heels sinking in the gravel, her crocodile skin green Hermes shoulder bag swinging in time with her bum. Her round muscled behind was outlined in a tight knee-length black-suede pencil skirt. Her bottom looked like two inflated footballs bouncing together in play.

Patrick watched for a short moment. That feeling of unbelievable luck in finding this new life surged through him. Yes, his new wife was unusual; changing his hairstyle, putting him in panties, the hair removal, expecting him to be naked around the home. All very strange, domineering. If that's what it took then it was what he would do.

He let himself out of the car, disappointed not to have had the same treatment as his wife. He took out Elizabeth's two enormous branded suitcases; they must have weighed over sixty pounds each. He placed them on the gravel next to his single plain blue suitcase.

"Mistress Elizabeth said for you to take her cases to the front room." Angie's elfin face looked mischievous as she left him there.

Patrick dragged his wife's heavy cases up the steps and into the wide front hall. Victorian black and white patterned tiles lay on the hall floor. In the front room to his right, Elizabeth sat in a single armchair scanning her post. Her personal assistant, Clara, stood next to her. Clara dealt with all of Elizabeth's non-business affairs and spent many hours at her home. Elizabeth had another assistant at her office, Charlotte, who dealt with her business affairs. Patrick liked the way his wife worked with the two ladies, with affection and friendship. Elizabeth was the boss but she was never overbearing with them.

The thought of exactly what Elizabeth had seen in him went through his mind as he watched his wife. Elizabeth had everything she wanted, didn't she? Except for a husband. With her lifestyle, that wasn't a necessity. He was missing something. What was it she wanted from him?

"Pat, take my bags up to my bedroom." Elizabeth didn't

look up from her letters. Clara nodded at him coolly and resumed working with his wife.

Patrick's body tightened at what had sounded like an order. It was her way but he felt more embarrassed with her doing it in front of others. And she had said *my* bedroom. That had changed now he was moving in. "Don't you mean our bedroom, Elizabeth?"

She ignored him, engrossed in her discussion with Clara.

He huffed, shook his head and lumbered the cases one at a time up the stairs to the first floor and the main bedroom. The bedroom never ceased to impress him. A king-sized plus bed sat in the middle of the enormous room. Stark white covers and soft high pillows covered the bed like a thick layer of fluffy snow. A deep embossed wallpaper was in off-white. Pictures of a long-lost English countryside hung around the high walls in clusters of two or three. In one corner, a partially open door led to an en-suite bathroom.

Opposite, another door was ajar revealing the walk-in wardrobe. It was as big as his bedroom at his previous apartment. He guessed the bedroom to be around forty-feet long and thirty wide. His feet sank into the thick lush carpet as he pulled her cases into the room.

He pushed the two suitcases against the wall and lay down on the end of the giant bed. He hung his feet off the end to avoid soiling the covers with his shoes. He sunk his head into the soft deep mattress beneath the down-filled duvet which wrapped itself around him. He pushed his nostrils into the thick Egyptian cotton covers. A smell of vanilla and roses filled his nose. Wonderful.

He remembered the first time they had made love in this bed. He had never had a woman take charge of lovemaking before, but he had laid back and enjoyed it all the same. A new experience. He imagined the evening lovemaking with his wife. If she stopped being in a bad mood. He was certain she would; now she was home. Elizabeth was a beautiful woman, despite her advancing years. And very wealthy, he didn't forget that part. It had been over a week since the last time they had sex. His balls ached for a release. Yes, it had been his fault — the champagne, the brandy. It had been too much of a temptation. Besides, there was plenty of time for sex with Elizabeth. For the next two years. He supposed that was partly the reason for her mood.

He closed his eyes and thought about the wedding. The marriage on the beach in the Maldives. Her executive assistant Charlotte had flown over to be her witness. The only other guests had been the Russian couple, their bodyguards and two seagulls who had insisted on perching on a lectern for the entire ceremony.

He smiled in the warm reminiscence at his joke during the ceremony. "I Patrick Hilary Ashleigh take you Elizabeth Margaret Remington, to be my wife. To have and to hold from this day forward, for better or for worse, for richer and for even richer." How he had giggled at replacing the word *poorer* with the words *even richer*."

Elizabeth hadn't got the joke. He didn't mind, he knew she didn't have a sense of humour. She was highly intelligent but she could never lighten up. Her lack of humour wasn't important. It was her money that meant everything. He snuggled down again rubbing his face into the fragrant cotton imagining the sex they would be having very soon.

"What are you doing, Pat?"

He sat up. Elizabeth stood framed in the doorway to the bedroom, hands on hips. The light from the landing window threw autumn sunlight around her head like a halo.

"Er, hello Elizabeth. I was relaxing on our bed."

No smile broke her face. Her eyes narrowed and bore down on him. He felt as if he were under the spotlight of interrogation. He would turn on his famous charm, it always worked and had worked with her, hadn't it? Once.

"I was imagining making slow sensual love to you in our bed, my darling." He leered.

She folded her arms below her huge breasts. His heart missed a beat at the sight of the low-cut cleavage. How he wanted to push his face into those breasts right now. Soft and luscious like the down-filled pillows on their bed.

"Get off my bed." Her face glared, reddened cheeks flushed. He jerked up.

"It's our bed now, dearest," he said, a silly grin across his sleepy face.

"It's *my* bed so get off or there will be trouble. And never call me dearest, do you understand me, Patty?"

She stood like an angry statue in the doorway. Stone-like and cold.

He jumped up. He had misread the tone. *Had she just called him Patty?* However, he thought it best to be a little more reticent. "We're married so it's now our bedroom and our bed. And why shouldn't I call my beautiful wife, *dearest*?"

He moved towards her, hands out to cuddle her. His charm and smile had always helped him out of problems with women and he would win this little fight, he thought. He never failed. He had never been with a woman as unusual as his new wife before but then he was confident she would come round to his way of thinking. Eventually.

She knew how to prolong a bad mood so he had to be pleasant. He would have access to all the wealth and luxury she had amassed. All he had to do was seem sympathetic and give her his 100-watt smile. He flashed his winning smile at Elizabeth and waited for her to melt.

Elizabeth scowled. Her ice wall remained. That wasn't in his internal script. What was wrong with this woman? How could she not be charmed by his looks and smile? Had he married a lesbian?

"Don't touch me." She spoke through clenched teeth and tightened lips.

He stepped back.

"You will only touch me when I allow it," she said.

He froze as if put into a freeze-frame from a hidden TV remote control. She was controlling him. "What?" he said with surprise.

"Follow me and I'll show you to *your* bedroom." She left the doorway with a flourish and her heels clomped down the landing. The thuds of her shoes muffled on the carpet like a dull crash. He would have to work a bit harder on his charm, this was going to be much more of a challenge than he'd anticipated. He had time though, she'd melt eventually. She couldn't keep this up forever.

For a short moment, he remained in his frozen position. He tried to compute what had happened, to process the information. *His bedroom?* He left the bedroom and his eyes flicked to where he had heard her walk. She was standing at the end of the long passage, arms folded again.

The passageway walls were covered in light, fine-patterned paper. At the end, on the left-hand side of the passage, a door was ajar. He glimpsed light-grey tiling and a rectangular white enamel sink. It had the hint of a Victorian style with the large chrome taps embossed on top with black H and C symbols. Elizabeth stood by a closed white door beyond the bathroom entrance.

He trudged towards his wife, the thick grey carpet made him feel as if he were walking through treacle. When was she going to come out of this mood? As he approached her, she glowered at him and she twisted the brass door handle with one hand. The door swung open and stood back. He peered inside.

A single bed with a plain white headboard sat in the centre of a small box room. It was a world away in size and style from what he had thought would be their bedroom. A light wooden double wardrobe with a half-length mirror was placed against one wall and a pine two-drawer bedside cabinet was set against the bed. A single reading lamp on the top was set alongside a digital clock; the red digits flashed 00:00. The room had the smell of new paint, carpet and cotton. His eyes wandered over the room. The walls were light pink. A purple duvet with a thin flowered pattern covered the bed. There was a plain but definite feminine touch to the décor.

"You'll be sleeping here, Patty. This is now your room."

His mouth opened and his forehead creased. She had to be joking. Elizabeth walked away leaving him aghast. He was sure about one thing. Elizabeth didn't do jokes.

Chapter 5 — The marriage contract

It was Sunday evening and Patrick was sitting at the dining table across from his wife; the strained ambience cracked in the air. Chinks and scrapes from their metal knives and forks on china plates broke through the chilly silence.

Outside a storm brewed. The clouds darkened and the sound of the wind whipping up fallen crisp-brown autumn leaves scrapped through from outside. Above the table, a glass chandelier threw a stark light onto the table. He shivered despite the warmth of the room.

Elizabeth sat at the head of the light wooden table, Two crossed thick table legs appeared to defy physics and gravity by holding the eight-foot-long table firm and steady. Elizabeth had spent Saturday out and all Sunday in her home office on the ground floor catching up on her business affairs. The only visitors coming and going into the house were her executive business assistant, Charlotte, and her personal assistant, Clara. Both were much younger than Elizabeth, but they worked with her in an easy comfortable manner. Almost like equals. Almost. She had a manner that made him think of her as if she were a head of state, a president or a queen. She sat aloof and alluring, full of power and authority. She looked beautiful and seductive. And infuriating.

That he had such a hot and wealthy wife, sustained him through this odd phase. Her mood had to change eventually. She couldn't keep this up. The only words they had exchanged all weekend had been that morning. He had got up from breakfast around 9 pm and she had already been up and about for three hours. She told him she would be working and that he knew how busy her business was and this was the life he had accepted.

That was true and worth the trouble. He had tried to give her a morning peck on the cheek which she had accepted without any acknowledgement or attempt to kiss him back. He hadn't expected to be sleeping in a separate bedroom from his wife on the first weekend back after their honeymoon.

It was true Elizabeth was a woman who expected to have her own way, she didn't accept debate. This was fine and he understood her manner but he knew he would have to bring up her current behaviour that evening over dinner. They had shared the bed in the hotel suite on the honeymoon. Why not now?

Elizabeth told him to remove his clothing for dinner. He stripped and left his clothes on the floor, feeling self-conscious as she flicked at her phone and appeared disinterested in him. She preferred him naked around the home and it was the first time she had asked him to strip off since they had returned from their honeymoon. He assumed this signified a return to normality, that's to say the kind of normality that existed in Elizabeth's mind.

She had only ever told him to be naked before when no one was around. Clara and Charlotte had been spending much of their time at the home that weekend so he guessed this was why she hadn't told him to be naked up to this point. They must have gone home for the evening. It would be just the two of them. Time to talk about her attitude.

They sat silently at the table. A Chinese delivery of plastic containers sat on the tabletop in open plastic containers. The familiar waft of oil and lemongrass rose into the air. After ten minutes of eating in silence, Elizabeth gave no indication she was going to start the conversation. Patrick squirmed with discomfort. It had been great to be naked when things were good, now it was uncomfortable. The thaw in their relationship hadn't happened after all. She was in a nice dress. It made him feel submissive and inferior.

He cleared his throat to attract her attention. "Elizabeth?"

She looked up from her food. Her eyes widened in anticipation, distracted, her mind elsewhere. He cleared his throat a second time. Summoning up some courage. He was uncomfortable at this situation. He pulled his legs together as his limp penis lay across his thigh and, thankfully, under cover of the tabletop. Even so, it was not a comfortable situation. He felt inferior and submissive.

"So, Elizabeth." He hesitated again as she chewed her food slowly, chopsticks hanging loosely from her fingers. She reminded him of a tiger chewing on its prey. "I don't understand what's going on. It's not the same, there's a bad atmosphere. I should get dressed."

He sat back. He was surprised to feel nervous, a sensation not helped by her ongoing silence and the frozen atmosphere. She placed her chopsticks on either side of her plate lining them up with precision. She looked at them for a moment and, satisfied they were straight, she glared up at him.

"No. You'll stay naked, Patty." She looked as if she was chewing something over in her mind. "I've been a little snowed under on coming back from our honeymoon so I haven't been able to deal with you. There's so much to catch up on when you run your own company."

Elizabeth picked up one chopstick and stabbed at a piece of half-eaten chicken. He jumped at the ferocity of her action.

Patrick wanted things in the open, although not his penis at this particular moment considering her current mood. "Why do you want us to sleep in separate bedrooms, Elizabeth? There's more to this, isn't there?"

Elizabeth was being uncharacteristically reticent. "Yes, Patty, there is something I need to say. It's a shame I had to wait so long but, as I said, my business comes first. Now I'm up to date, I can get round to you."

Patrick put his cutlery down, he'd never mastered chopsticks. They were too fussy, too difficult to shovel food into his mouth. Their conversation hung in the air like a bad smell. This was not going well. He was sure he was not going to like what she was about to say.

"Go on," he said, nerves jangling. He wished he'd not undressed. What could she have done anyway if he had not complied?

Elizabeth fixed her face into her cool business mode. "It's like this." Her confidence showed in her upright back, like a ballet dancer's. "You signed the pre-nuptial agreement. You agreed it was fair that in the event of a divorce, you have no claim on what I have built up myself. You would get nothing from our marriage financially."

Patrick nodded. He hadn't read the document properly but wasn't too worried. He would have access to all her luxury and wealth by default. He had it all worked out. He didn't plan to divorce her immediately so what was the problem? After a couple of years in a senior position in her business, he would challenge the prenuptial and show he had contributed.

Even if he only got a million pounds out of a future court case or, more likely, an out-of-court settlement, that would not be a bad return for two years investment in the marriage. Besides, she was pretty hot for an older woman, it wasn't going to be too tough. Win-win. Or it will be once she snapped out of her rotten mood. What was wrong with her? She knew how to string a bad temper on for days. He had never expected that of her.

Elizabeth continued. "I guessed you wouldn't read the document properly so I inserted a separate contract to the pre-nuptial."

His grin fell away like melting snow. Now she had his full attention.

He leant forward, fingers grasping the tabletop. "What contract?" A hot flush rose from his neck." What contract?" he repeated, betraying his rising panic.

"An employment-type contract that states you agree to obey me. If you don't obey me, our marriage becomes null and void and you get nothing. You waived all rights to be an equal in our marriage. It means legally, I lead the marriage and make all the decisions. You have also waived the right to anything from me. Not a bean. You signed an agreement to not go to court for anything, even if you helped to generate income during our marriage. A pre-nuptial only covers me financially. You signed two documents, the pre-nuptial and the contract. To be more precise, it was an employment contract. Legally, you are also my employee as well as my husband."

He rubbed the back of his neck then pushed his fingers through his hair.

"The definition in the contract you didn't bother to read is you renounce the right to anything. There are no exceptions. So if I tell you to stand on the table and dance, you do it. If I tell you to wiggle your arse for me, you do it. If I tell you to clean the toilet with your tongue, you do it. Failure to do what I order is a breach of contract and you will be expelled from my house instantly. That includes clothing of course. Or lack of *herewith*." Her legalise was a sharp reminder of the contract ruse. "The marriage will become null and void if you ever misbehave. For example, if you had refused to be naked tonight, it would have been a breach of contract."

He gulped and his mouth dropped open. "Why did you marry me, Elizabeth?"

"Why did you marry me, Patrick?" She let her question hang. "As for me, I wanted a good-looking pliable younger man on tap for my personal use. To serve me and do whatever I want you to do. A kind of manservant. I also don't just want sex with only one man." She looked to the ceiling. "That's so boring. I want to be able to continue to bring back lovers, one-night stands. Whatever I feel like. I don't want to have a jealous husband complaining. I want a jealous husband *not* complaining. I find the whole cuckold scene exciting. If I had merely employed you, I'm sure you would have become fed-up after a few weeks. I needed utter control of you, Patty. Now you can't leave until I decide you are not doing what I want. I can then fabricate an excuse and you'd be gone. Without me losing a penny."

Patrick stood up. He banged the table with a fist. He lost himself for a moment. "That's not fair, you tricked me." His anger was tempered by his knowledge he had entered the marriage for money and what he thought he could get from her in a couple of years. She had check-mated him. He had lost and was boxed into a corner. She had been too clever for him. He was standing angry and naked. His flaccid penis hung loose. Elizabeth shot it a glance and grimaced. He sat back down quickly, flustered.

She hadn't finished. "Listen to this, *Patty,* and then tell me I was unfair."

He cringed at her continued use of the feminine version of his name again as she fished in a handbag by her feet. She pulled out a black hand-held plastic device and laid it on the table between them.

"I record all my calls for business reasons, even on holiday. I attached a voice recorder to our hotel room phone line. I heard your calls to Mike. I felt something wasn't right with you. You were a little too easy. Normally my men have been a bit of a challenge, but you never were. Why was that, I thought? Now I know. You married me so you could take my money."

Patrick's mouth dropped open. She had him.

"You were always perfect malleable material for my needs. Now you're utterly under my control, how delightful. You may be good looking but you're a little slow on the uptake."

Patrick's stomach turned over. He thought he might be sick. She flicked on the recorder. He heard himself telling his best friend Mike how he had won the lottery of life. How he could never love an old woman like Elizabeth, but he loved the idea he would have money and a celebrity business wife. He was going to be rich and comfortable once he divorced her. Now they had married he would take over and do as he pleased. Then after two years he would fabricate a divorce and walk away as a rich man.

He cringed. He tried to speak but nothing came out. He had nothing to say. No excuse. He was trapped. If only he'd read that damn contract.

Elizabeth's finger clicked on the pause button and put a stop to his nightmare. "Do I need to play any more of this, or do you see what is going to happen? Are you bright enough to see that, Patty?"

Patrick's head went down. Humiliated and condemned by his own recorded words.

Elizabeth continued. "It's not the end of the world for you

though. If you behave and do as I say then you can live comfortably, more or less. Until I get bored with you. I did have a little pang of concern about why I wanted to marry you, but after I heard that call you made that all blew away. Like your plans, Patty. Now I can go even further than I had originally planned. I can do whatever I want to you and you can do nothing about it, *Patty*. You're still good base material for my needs, I need to keep an eye on you. That shouldn't be too difficult, you're not the smartest blade in the box, are you? *Patty?*"

Patrick wiped away beads of sweat from his forehead with the back of his hand. *Was it hot in here?* He didn't think so. He wasn't as stupid as Elizabeth had painted him, was he? She was smarter, that much was clear.

"You'll still need to work for me of course. Report to me on Monday morning at my head office in Shoreditch, 9 am. I'll be getting there earlier of course but 9 is fine for you."

Patrick relaxed. This was his chance. He would show her what a great businessman he could be. Maybe he wasn't as clever as her but he would be diligent and work hard to make her business a success. Maybe she would forgive him in time. Then he could pounce and get her money. There was still a chance.

"Yes, of course, Elizabeth," he said. "I'm looking forward to showing you how good a businessman I am. I'll show you. We can put all of this behind us and find real affection. We have to work at it Elizabeth." He felt fired up and desperate, almost believing his own lies. This was his opportunity to get a way back into her respect. "I made a mistake Elizabeth but I was drunk. I didn't mean what I said to Mike. I promise I'll be a good husband for you. We will work together to make the company even more successful. And we'll work on making our marriage a success too. Let's move on from this, Elizabeth."

A faint grin spread across Elizabeth's lips. "I'm sure you will be an extremely useful employee in my company and a good little hubby at home. The girls in my office will love having you around."

Patrick felt a little more relaxed now. His easy charm and great looks would win over the ladies at Elizabeth's company, *no problemo*. He thought about giving her his special smile but thought better of it after its previous failure. He was warming to the discussion now.

"I thought it would be great for me to bring a male perspective to your organisation. It must be a little restrictive having an all-female top team?"

Elizabeth looked momentarily bemused. Patrick took it as a good sign. "Actually, Patty, all my employees are female and I want to keep it this way."

"What?" he said. That didn't make sense. He was going to be working there now. He brushed the thought away, she must be confused and heady at her plan coming together. Patrick bounced slightly on his chair in his enthusiasm. "What role do you have in mind for me? I'm very creative, that's why I was a musician. Maybe I could be Vice President of your marketing department? Or maybe...." She cut him short with a raised hand. He stopped what he was saying.

Elizabeth's face dropped. Serious. Her eyes narrowed. "Enough discussion. Report to my office on Monday morning and then you'll find out exactly what I consider to be the most suitable role for you."

Why had she said that with such venom?

Chapter 6 — His wife's the boss

Patrick paced the floor of the lobby of his wife's company. Thirty minutes after he had been told to arrive, he was still waiting. He hadn't even got past the ground-floor reception desk. His cheeks were flushed red, his breathing rapid. He snorted hard through his nostrils and sat down and got up again. He put his hands in his dark-grey suit trousers.

He glanced at the mirrored walls; he looked good. He relaxed a little. The made-to-measure light-grey Italian suit Elizabeth had bought him for the honeymoon clung to him like a tailored glove. The jacket added width through the padding to his narrow sloping shoulders. Sharp-creased trousers finished on brightly polished black leather shoes. Padded out, of course, to give the appearance of a broad back.

He had swept back his long black hair with wet-look gel that morning. It had the semblance of a quiff and curled over the white collar of his fitted shirt, flowing onto the tops of his shoulders. Maybe a little longer than he would have chosen but overall, he looked damn good; like a successful businessman. He turned sideways on to the mirrors. He decided the longer hair Elizabeth wanted wasn't bad; it made him look cool, like an Italian.

The reception area was contemporary and sterile. Elizabeth's company occupied all five floors of the renovated former industrial red-brick building. Through the smoked glass front doors, he watched the heavy morning traffic snarl its way past. Black taxis and red double-deckers disgorged and picked up busy passengers. People strutted past on the pavements. Everyone seemed in a hurry to be somewhere else. He turned away. Soon he would be calling the shots here at the company. Maybe he would make the reception more welcoming as a first move? He would shake things up and make his mark. He'd soon show his wife how good he was. He'd had no business training but so what? How hard could it be? He'd give things a fresh new look.

The young man at the reception desk wore a dark-blue uniform. He thought Elizabeth had said all her employees were female. The receptionist was polite to him in a passive-aggressive manner when he had complained he was the CEO's husband and shouldn't be kept waiting.

The female employees entered the lobby and waved their electronic pass cards at the waist-high security gates that opened at their command. He thought about vaulting over the barriers but remembered his wife's words on Sunday night about obeying. He thought it best to not antagonise her. Not yet, not until the incident she had recorded faded from memory. His success at the office would win her round. She would put his indiscretion on the honeymoon to one side, he was sure. Then he could get back to his original plan once again. Wait two years, divorce and get her money. The stupid contract she'd tricked him with could be challenged in court.

He didn't immediately spot the smart young lady who appeared next to him like a ghost. He felt her presence and smelt her perfume first, then her voice. "Mr Remington?"

He spun around. The lady's shoulder-length blond hair moved in one wave as she tilted her head to one side. It was like an advert for a shampoo commercial, he thought. A pass card with her photo and name hung around her neck on a black lanyard. It nestled above her breasts which were covered by a high-necked white blouse done up to her neck in a tight prim manner. Her taut drawn face stared hard at him. A black pencil skirt hugged her trim thighs and finished just above her knees.

His first reaction was she needed some sun on her pasty white face. Vibrant red lipstick looked like a scar against her white sheet-like skin.

"Er no," he said. "That's my wife's maiden name. I'm Patrick Ashleigh."

She pondered his reply for an instant. "I'm Lindsay Forrest, Mrs Remington's Head of HR. Follow me, Mr Remington." She strutted towards the barriers.

He stumbled after her, off-guard, tripping slightly in his efforts to follow. "No...er, wait. I'm Mr Ashleigh. Remington is my wife's previous name. Before we married. Ms Forrest..."

Lindsay Forrest appeared not to hear him as she approached the security barriers. She tilted down to touch the pad with her pass card and the clear glass barriers slid aside. Patrick gaped at her pert bum, outlined against the tight skirt.

She turned back at that instant, their eyes locked and he tore them away. He felt his cheek burn.

"This way, Mr Remington." She said without dropping her cool unblinking eyes.

"No, no, you've got it wrong," he said, staggering after her. "I'm Mr Ashleigh. Ms Forrest? Are you listening to me?"

Lindsay Forrest walked as if her head was held erect by invisible strings. Her heels clipped on the tiled floor. She got to the lifts and pressed the call button three times with impatience. Her eyes rolled to the ceiling and she breathed out noisily.

Patrick caught her up. "Lindsay, Ms Forrest, I don't think you heard me. My surname is Ashleigh. You see my wife kept her maiden name: Remington. I'm Mr Ashleigh."

Lindsay Forrest fixed her gaze on him. Her eyes dropped down his body then up again as if working him out and deciding he wasn't that good. A look of distaste flitted across her lips. "I heard you perfectly well, Mr Remington." The lift pinged to announce its arrival and the doors swished open. Ms Forrest stepped in. "Follow me, *Mr Remington.*"

He sighed and sloped into the lift. Reflective black plastic lined the interior. He caught his darkened reflection and touched and tousled his hair with a hand. Looking great, he thought. A smarmy grin flitted across his face; the female employees in his wife's company would be putty in his hand. He would knock them out, using his charm to get what he wanted. Maybe not Lindsay 'hard-face' Forrest, she had a problem. But the others? They would fall at his fee. He may not be the musical troubadour right now, but as a Senior Vice President, the sky was the limit to his sexual success here. His wife's remoteness since the honeymoon would not stop him.

He stretched himself to his full height behind the prim Lindsay Forrest. He would become the power behind his wife's throne and Lindsay Forrest would have to fall into line. He'd put a stop to her snooty ways. What women like her needed was a good seeing to. He smiled to himself.

The lift stopped with a bounce and the doors swished open onto a modern 4th-floor office. A bustle of activity hit him. A swarm of businesswomen moved around, working at desks, carrying papers, folders and heading to meetings. The large room was full of desks, PC screens and glass partitions. He stepped out of the lift, following the pinch-faced Lindsay Forrest.

"You will be referring to me as Ms Forrest from now on. Do you understand me, Mr Remington?" she said while strutting towards the far side of the room.

Ms Forrest? Who did she think she was? His wife was the CEO of the whole company and him, as the man, was effectively the real boss despite the Vice President title. *Ms Forrest* indeed, he guessed she was a little confused as to the situation. Ms Lindsay Forrest was *his* employee.

Ms Forrest told him to sit in a meeting room in the corner of the large open room. She pointed the way with a slim white index finger. He trudged over and went in. A table dominated the room, leaving little room around it. It was made of highly polished wood almost like a glass surface. It reflected back his face, distorted like a caricature.

Six chairs surrounded the table. A massive flat-screen hung on the only wall not made of glass. Aluminium Venetian blinds closed the room off from the main office. He peered out of the outside windows to the skyline around him. The imposing dome of St Paul's cathedral drew his eyes from between the more recent oddly-shaped office buildings, each with a nickname: the Gherkin, the Walkie-Talkie, the Shard. In the distance, the grand towers of Tower Bridge loomed beyond the turrets of the Tower of London. A place for traitors to be imprisoned in past times. How he'd like to put *Ms Forrest* in there.

It was a great view from the 4th floor. It would be a nice place to work. The 4th floor. A thought hit him, Elizabeth's office was on the 5th Floor, why was he on the 4th?

Chapter 7 — The office junior

Patrick stepped away from the window and glanced back into the main office to see Ms Forrest striding towards him. She had a much younger lady by her side. The lady had brown hair, brown-rimmed glasses and carrying a cardboard folder against her chest. He guessed she was no more than twenty-three years old. His eyes fell on her long legs and gathered flowing purple mini skirt. The two women entered the room.

He put both hands onto the table, leaning towards them. He had to show her who was boss. "Ms Forrest, where's my wife? I demand to see her right now." That sounded good. Very Vice Presidential.

The two women looked at each other. The younger lady shut the door behind her and it clicked smoothly into place.

Ms Forrest observed like a school teacher with a naughty pupil. "Mr Remington, please sit."

He felt anger rumble inside him. She had continued to call him by his wife's surname. "I want to see my wife right now, *Lindsay Forrest*. I'm here to start work with her in a senior management position." He stood upright and pulled on his jacket lapels like a lawyer summing up in court. "I'm extremely creative and I have several ideas to discuss with her about improving revenues." He narrowed his eyes. "And improving our subordinates' attitudes." He allowed his glare to linger on Ms Forrest for a few moments. She remained impassive. "I know it will seem strange to you I appear to be reporting to my wife, but that's just for appearances. In reality, I will have full autonomy. As a man, I'm actually be the one in charge. Of course, I'm sure you understand." He nodded to himself, resting his case. That should tell the pompous *Ms* Forrest who's who.

The two ladies looked at each other. The younger lady put a hand to her lips and stifled a giggle. How strange. He would deal with her insubordination later.

"So where's Elizabeth?" he asked, head swivelling between the two.

They shared a look again. The young lady pushed back on her glasses and pulled her folder tighter to her chest. He had to let them know who was in charge and then work on this delightful lady later. "Hello?" He knocked on the table sarcastically. "My wife? Elizabeth? Where is she?" His voice raised.

Ms Forrest tensed. A flash of anger showed in her small steel-coloured eyes. The first emotion he'd seen in her. "Ms Remington is in a meeting on the 5th Floor. She's extremely busy."

"I'm sure she is, but take me to her and I'll wait. Tell her that her husband, Mr *Ashleigh,* is waiting. Now, if you don't mind, *Lindsay Forrest,*" he said, shooing her away with a sweep of his fingers.

The friction in the room sparked around like a broken high-voltage cable in a hurricane.

"Mr Remington." Ms Forrest took a deep breath to calm herself. "It's only because you *are* Mrs Remington's husband that I am accepting your poor behaviour. For the moment. To be clear, Mrs Remington gave me instructions as to what she wanted from you, including what surname you are to use."

Her words took the wind from his swagger. A dagger of doubt thrust into his chest. "What do you mean?"

Ms Forrest visibly relaxed as she detected the first signs of his arrogance falling away. "She told me she had no reason to meet with you as Jackie Swann." She opened a palm towards the young lady with the short skirt. "Will be more than able to guide you in your new job here.

"I, I, I don't understand," he stammered. His head swam full of confusion. Who was this silly young girl? Jackie Swann? She was just a child. What was going on here?

"It's very simple, Mr Remington. Ms Swann is your line manager and she will instruct you as to your tasks here. What's so difficult about that?" Exasperation leaked into Ms Forrest's words. She fought to retain a level of professional demeanour. Jackie Swann looked nervous, this was not what she had expected.

Patrick looked around as if trying to find the strength. "What do you mean *Ms* Swann will be my line manager? She's barely out of school. I'm a Vice President here."

Jackie Swann bristled and seemed to extend her height by a couple more inches. She pushed her glasses back on her nose. She looked more like a secretary than his line manager.

Jackie swallowed. "Mr Remington, Pat. I have no idea what you're talking about. You're not a Vice President. Ms Remington told me you're to start work as the Administration Assistant. You'll be reporting to me and responsible for general office duties." She looked at Ms Forrest for reassurance. Ms Forrest nodded back to confirm

"Don't talk rubbish, girl." He glared at Jackie then turned to look at Ms Forrest. Her lips pursed as if she wanted to spit at him. His face burnt bright red. "Get me my wife now or nothing is going to happen."

"I see you're going to be difficult, Pat," Jackie said.

"Don't call me Pat. I'm Mr Ashleigh to you. I'm a Vice President, the company CEO's husband." He pointed at Jackie Swann while fixing eye contact with Ms Forrest. "And get this stupid girl out of here and back to her secretarial duties."

Ms Forrest took Jackie by the arm and led her out of the room, leaving the door open. That had got their attention. This must be a case of mistaken identity. He breathed in hard and fast. Gasping at the audacity of these two stupid women. Can't they get anything right. How hard was it to greet the new Vice

President appropriately. He would sack them both later today. Before lunch.

Outside the meeting room, Ms Forrest was on her mobile phone. Her lips moved silently from the other side of the glass wall. She shook with rage, a red patch glowing on her pale neck. Ms Forrest hung up and she and Jackie sat at a desk outside the room. They seemed to be waiting.

Patrick stomped around the meeting room table. He clenched his fists tight. He tried to calm down.

"How dare they speak to me like that? It must be a mistake," he said to himself. "Who did they think they were? Ms Forrest will be facing the sack. Even with a case of mistaken identity they had no right to treat me like this." He faced towards the grey October city skyline. "I can't believe it. When I speak to Elizabeth they will be both sacked, dismissed. I will see to it. This will all work out for me. They will be dismissed. The two of them."

He relaxed, watching a bird swirling in the thermals outside the window. He thought to himself, what could go wrong? His wife was the company CEO.

Chapter 8 — The new junior admin girl

"The only person likely to be dismissed is you, Patty."

He spun around. He hadn't heard anyone come in. Elizabeth stood in the doorway composed, arms on hips. Her breasts pushed out large and firm from a tight white blouse. She entered the room. Ms Forrest and Jackie Swann followed behind her. Elizabeth was snarling.

"Elizabeth, you have two very poor employees here. I suggest we get rid of them now."

Elizabeth glared at him as he continued. "Who do they think they are? Ms Jackie *just-out-of-school* Swann is probably the most junior person in the company." He snorted.

A smirk trickled up one side of Elizabeth's lips. "No Patty, Jackie Swann is the *second* most junior person here." She stared hard. "You're the most junior."

His mouth opened and closed. He was confused. What was going on? His wife had just called him Patty again in front of these women. He had assumed it was her pet name for him, but it sounded too feminine. He was uncomfortable. Confused.

"Patty, I'm busy and I was in an important meeting with my senior managers. I don't have time to deal with the junior office staff problems. You will do what Jackie tells you because I asked her to be your line manager. You are not a Vice President, you are the Admin. Assistant to all the ladies on this floor. You're to do whatever they tell you to do. I'm not giving you a Vice President role, what on earth were you thinking? Now before I go I want to hear you apologise to Jackie and Lindsay and tell them what a naughty boy you've been. If not, you're out of here and out of my home. Remember the contract you signed?" She waited, arms crossed again.

His mind raced, this was flying at him as if he were in a nightmare. He would wake up soon, wouldn't he? What should he do? Elizabeth's long talon-like nails tapped on the tabletop as she leant towards him. Tap, tap, tap. A ticking time bomb to humiliation.

"I'm waiting, Patty," Elizabeth said. "Admin. Assistant or out on the street?"

There it was again: *Patty*. The diminutive, the feminine.

He was cornered. It was best to apologise and think of a way around this little snag. Maybe Elizabeth was testing him? Maybe it was her idea of a joke? No, that was unlikely, she didn't do jokes. Apologise and then see what happens. Patrick swallowed hard. Apologies didn't come easy, especially when he didn't know what was going on. He looked down. "I'm sorry, ladies," he mumbled.

"Louder, Patty, and look at them when you're saying it. I want to hear you say you're sorry for being rude to them."

Patrick's face flushed and burned red. This was a level of humiliation he had never experienced before. Apologise was not a word in his vocabulary. Apologising to two women was not in his internal code.

Elizabeth stood up. She'd had enough. "I don't have the time for this. Patty, leave the building, go home, pack your things and go. It's over."

He looked at her, astonished. She was serious. This wasn't a joke or a test. What had happened to her, what was going wrong? He had no job, no house. She had tricked him. "Elizabeth, please." He pleaded as she stomped towards the door.

"Last chance. Apologise." Her reply came as she held open the door for him to leave

He looked across at the two ladies. "I'm very sorry for my behaviour, ladies." His head fell.

A smile of success swiped over Elizabeth's face. "That wasn't so hard was it, Patty?"

He thought he ought to reply. "No, Elizabeth."

"No, Ms Remington," Elizabeth replied.

Patrick didn't understand. Why was she saying Ms Remington to him?

Elizabeth walked over and put an index finger under his chin and lifted his head. "You will address me as Ms Remington. Who do you think you are? You're a lowly Admin. Assistant and I'm the company CEO." She glanced across at Ms Forrest. "Lindsay, some of the staff these days don't understand manners do they?"

Ms Forrest smirked and shook her head. Jackie Swann played with her glasses as she watched everything with surprised fascination.

Elizabeth turned her attention back to the shocked Patrick. "If you misbehave any more, I'll be taking down your trousers and underpants, putting you over my knee and spanking you." She glared without blinking.

This was a step too far. She had gone beyond humiliation. "Now Elizabeth what on earth are you…"

He never got to finish his sentence as Elizabeth moved towards him and slapped him across the face. With a swift twirl, she pulled him over her lap. She sat on the chair at the same time, pulling him with her. He fell face-first over her knees.

"Help me hold him, ladies," said Elizabeth.

Ms Forrest and Jackie Swan shot across the room. Ms Forrest held his head down and Jackie held his legs. Elizabeth ripped at his trousers and pulled them down with his underpants to his shoes. His bare bum was exposed. His penis lay across her stockinged thighs. This couldn't be happening, he thought. This is unreal.

Elizabeth threw a stinging slap across his bum cheeks. It echoed around the meeting room, bouncing off the glass walls.

Slap, down came her hand again. Patrick called out for her to stop as she rained spanks on his reddening bum cheeks — slap, slap, slap, slap. He was being spanked by his wife. Her two employees were watching and helping. Utter humiliation.

Elizabeth continued to spank him. His trousers and underpants hung around his ankles, his shirt was pushed up and around his chest. Lindsay Forrest held his head and Jackie's arms were clamped around his legs. He felt her breasts pressed on his thighs.

He tried to push his legs out and up but Jackie Swann had them in a vice-like grip. He was trapped. His bum was sore.

"Oh look ladies, his bum is bright red and warm. Feel it." Two hands rubbed against his bum cheeks.

Elizabeth rubbed his sore bum gently. This was nice. A tingle shot through his penis then it burst into life between his wife's knees. Elizabeth pushed him off her knees and onto the floor. Patrick sat up, his erection raging between his legs. His hands flashed down to cover it. He stayed like that for a few moments. He closed his knees together. Everything was falling apart around him. His world had come crashing around him in a surreal fashion.

His new wife had pulled down his trousers and underpants and spanked his bare bottom in front of two employees. What was going on? The ladies watched, Jackie Swann's eyes filled with astonishment at his barely concealed penis and balls between his fingers. His erection was strong and throbbing.

Elizabeth stood, her hands moving to her hips again. This meant more trouble. She looked down at him. "Well, well. You're enjoying this. That makes it much easier."

"Elizabeth, what is wrong with you?" He complained, hands tight against his erection, knees pulled in. "How could you?"

"Stand up, Patty," came her reply.

He pushed himself up unsteadily. One hand over his penis and balls the other pushing himself up off the floor. He stood up, his trousers and underpants around his ankles. He bent down to pull them up.

"Uh uh. No you don't." Elizabeth wagged a finger at him. I was going to find new clothes for you in time but we might as well do it now. Step out of your shoes, socks and trousers."

"Changed? What do you mean?" He looked around at the three women. Jackie Swann shrugged her shoulders, her eyes flitting down to his erection fighting to escape from between its curtain of fingers.

Elizabeth nodded to Ms Forest who strode out of the room. Prim and stiff. Jackie remained in the room, looking incredulously at him.

Elizabeth's hands went again to her hips. "I had been hoping this would have been easier. You could have gone to a changing room to put on your new clothes but no, you had to make things difficult. As usual. Oh well, however we do it, the result was always going to be the same. Now, clothes off."

"What are you talking about, Elizabeth? What new clothes?" He felt ridiculous standing there with his wife.

Elizabeth moved back. "Clothes off, Patty." She nodded to Jackie.

Jackie knelt and undid his shoelaces and slipped his shoes and socks off. She pulled her head away from proximity to his erection. Elizabeth unbuttoned his shirt. His eyes flicked to the office door. There was no one in sight, that was some relief, his humiliation was restricted to these three women.

"Wait," he said with a weak voice. "Isn't this illegal? You can't strip an employee at work. That's sexual harassment."

Jackie Swann had pulled one trouser leg off from under his foot as Elizabeth removed his shirt. Jackie took his trousers and underwear off from around his other foot. He was naked. He covered his erection and balls as best he could with his fingers but it was too erect. She had humiliated him. She had got her revenge for the overheard phone call to his best friend. This would be enough.

He had taken his punishment and accepted it. Now they could move on. They would all stand there for a few moments and then he would get dressed. He knew he wouldn't be her Vice President now but he would knuckle down and do what was necessary for a couple of years. Then the big divorce. He would cite her cruelty and humiliation in court. He'd make a diary of this.

His mind came back to the present as Elizabeth put her face into his. "The junior admin. *girl* doesn't get to wear sharp Italian men's suits. She doesn't get to wear expensive fitted shirts either. No, *she* wears something far more appropriate to *her* role."

Patrick had no idea what she was talking about. He thought it best to allow her this moment of vengeance and then move on. The whole morning had been a nightmare wrapped in a horror show. Now his wife was talking in riddles. Of course a female admin. assistant doesn't wear a male business suit, she'd have a pretty dress or skirt. What did that have to do with him?

Chapter 9 — A pretty skirt

Elizabeth sighed for a few moments. Her waving hair was swept back and over her shoulders. He thought for a moment she looked great, which was an odd thing to come into his mind. She flicked her hair with a shake of her head. She was enjoying herself. That made her all the more alluring.

"Is this game over now, Elizabeth?" said Patrick despairingly.

"You'll call me Ms Remington, Patty."

"Don't be ridiculous, you're my wife."

"And you're my junior employee, the office *girl*. If you don't address me correctly I'll have you disciplined for your poor attitude."

Ms Forrest re-entered the room at that moment, holding a hanger, a pink blouse hung from it. Inside the blouse, a short pleated skirt in a darker pink shade hung from two thin black straps. Another surreal moment had arrived. The Head of HR was holding up girls' clothing. Young girls' clothing. He shook his head, this must all be some kind of a dream. A nightmare. Yes, that was it. He was dreaming, he was still on his honeymoon sleeping off a free champagne and cocktail hangover.

He squeezed his eyes tight then opened them again as Ms Forrest removed the blouse and skirt from the hanger and passed them to his wife. Elizabeth was smirking. She threw the clothes onto the table. They slid smoothly across the surface towards him.

"Put the pretty clothes on, Patty. After that, your manager, Ms Swann, will show you your new job."

It wasn't a dream or a nightmare it was real. His wife was staring him in the face telling him to put on a skimpy skirt and a female blouse. In pink!

Elizabeth spoke to Lindsay Forrest and Jackie. "You can take it from here, ladies. Any problems let me know and we'll put *her* on a disciplinary warning. If that happens we will have to suspend her and send her home in her new clothes."

Patrick pulled the clothing from the table and pulled it across his erection. The soft sheer fabric of the skirt felt smooth and erotic against his skin. This wasn't going to be easy.

Elizabeth left the meeting room and glided to the lift. The room hung in difficult silence.

Jackie moved down next to him. She touched his arm, a tingle in his skin. "We got off to a bad start, Patty." She smiled sweetly. "Why don't you slip on the pretty skirt and top and we can make a start on your jobs."

"I'll leave you to sort her out, Jackie. Call me if she continues to misbehave." Ms Forrest then left the room, carrying Patrick's male clothing across an arm. He watched her with helplessness, carrying his masculinity out of the door.

Jackie sat on a meeting room chair next to Patrick. He didn't know what to do. He held the skirt and blouse across his erection. Jackie crossed her legs, his eyes were drawn to them. Her flowing light purple skirt slid up her thigh and hung towards the floor from her seat. The light from the window shimmered on her glossy tan stockings. Jackie's large eyes were magnified slightly by her lenses. She blinked long lashes covered in black mascara. She wore an air of young innocent naivety. He might be able to play on that naivety. She tousled her long hair with her fingers, twisting the strands into nervous plaits. Neither of them knew what to do or say.

"Patty?" she said, then stopped.

"It's Patrick, actually," he shot back.

"I know but Lindsay and Ms Remington told me I should call you Patty and that you were to report to me. I'd expected you to be more open to what they had told me was going to happen. Elizabeth said she wanted you feminised and you wanted this too." She appeared to be on the verge of tears. She continued, her eyes becoming even larger. "They told me that you wanted to wear female clothes and that you would do anything I asked. I didn't expect you to struggle." She looked down, averting his astonished gaze. She looked up again. Was her innocence real or contrived?

"Well, I don't want to wear girls' clothes and I don't want to work for you either."

Jackie sniffed, his comment hit her confidence. Her large bosom twitched in her low-cut white tee-shirt top. His eyes lingered on her cleavage a moment too long before he dragged them away.

"I'm on probation, Patty. If I don't succeed and you take advantage of my inexperience, they won't give me a new contract. So please help me and put the little skirt and blouse on. Please. For me? It's not as if you have anything else to wear, is it? Lindsay took your male clothes away." She looked up at him, a pleading in her eyes. There was something else behind those glasses. He was not certain but behind the outward innocent naivety, was it possible she was enjoying this?

He didn't care about this girl or her games. In the past, he would have swatted her aside like an annoying fly. This situation was different and her point was true: he was naked and with only girls' clothing to put on. He stood, keeping the skirt and blouse firmly over his penis. The material was nice, soft and erotic. He didn't want that to distract him.

In the last few minutes, his erection had gone down. But what could he do about this bizarre situation? He looked again at her pleading eyes. Was there a tear? At least she wasn't as rude as Elizabeth or as cold as that horrible frigid Ms Forrest.

Jackie inspected her bright red fingernails, despair written hard on her face. "Please get dressed in the skirt and blouse. For me? Do what I ask and then you can discuss this whole odd situation with your wife later tonight. But for today, please do it. I need the job, I need the money. I need the success."

She reached out to his hand. Was she acting? She looked genuinely concerned but there was something else. She was a lady showing him some kindness and care for the first time in some time. She rubbed her thumb against the back of his hand. Goosebumps ran down his arm and up his neck. What was there to lose? Jackie hadn't done anything wrong and he guessed she was being genuine. It was Ms Forrest and his increasingly nasty wife who were the enemy. Jackie was only doing what they had told her to do. She had no choice.

"OK," he said. He turned his back and pulled on the little pink skirt in a flurry of thumbs and fingers. He felt stupid as he turned back to face her. He pulled at the skirt to make the elasticated waistband rest on his hips. Any higher and the end of his penis would show beneath the hem. The ghost of a triumphant smile flicked across Jackie's lips. He pulled on the blouse and buttoned it. Jackie stood and faced him. She straightened his blouse for him and pulled it outside the skirt. "It looks nicer this way." She smiled.

"Why are you calling me a girl?" He asked as he fought a stiffening of his penis. It peeked below the hem. Being called a girl had excited him, but he hated it. What were these feelings he was having?

His exposed erect penis head caught Jackie's eye. A wide grin came over her face as she ignored his question. "Oh look you're excited by your little skirt. I'm so pleased that you like it. This makes things easier." She moved in and gave him a little hug and a brief peck on the cheek. The brush of her skirt against the end of his penis caused it to jerk erect.

"I don't like the skirt," he snorted, but her words and the hug had ratcheted up his excitement as he tried to fight against his swelling penis.

It was a losing battle. His humiliation was exhilarating. The feel of his soft mini skirt against his genitals and Jackie's close presence. He smelled her sweet perfume. He felt heady as if he were drunk and battered. She studied him standing in the little pink mini skirt with his erection exposed beneath the hem. Jackie stood back and nodded as his erection stood out firm and hard, pointing upwards. The skirt had slid along the stem exposing it fully. He pulled the hem over his penis, pushing it sideways to avoid showing.

She pulled his hands away, whispering, "No, it's cute." Her perfume pervaded his senses again. "It's nice to see it like that. I like the mix of femininity and erection." She put a hand over her mouth as she giggled.

"Can I have some underwear? Please? Or a longer skirt?" He tried to ignore her comments as they formed a knot of arousal in his stomach.

Jackie's face took on a more serious note as she gave it some thought. "Lindsay and Ms Remington never said anything about underwear, they only said you were to wear this. I don't want to get into trouble. It's best you wear only what they gave you."

Jackie smiled again. She seemed sweet, she was his only option for any help. He tugged at the hem of his skirt again trying to cover his erection. Jackie brushed his hands away once more. "Let it hang naturally, Patty. It's nice to see it framed around a pink skirt. Cute. Pretty. There's little you can do about it if you're hard so let it be. We've all seen an erection before."

Her words hit his brain like a hammer. We. The entire office was about to see him this way.

Jackie took his hand. "Come on silly, let's get this over with. Once everyone sees you they will get used to it. Ms Remington told us all earlier that you would be coming today as a transvestite so no one will be shocked." She thought a moment. "Maybe they didn't expect to see you with a raging erection but it is what it is. Hard." She giggled behind a hand. "Our all-woman office has to learn to accept diversity and a man who identifies as a woman."

He wanted to say that he didn't identify as a woman but he was disorientated. This young lady was being kind in her own way. Perhaps he had misjudged her. She was sweet. She squeezed his hand tighter as if to say, trust me and I'll look after you. It was comforting. He looked down at the floor. His erection pointed up to the ceiling, the little skirt hem laying on the base. His balls hung loose and visible.

"I should cover up, Jackie. Maybe they believe I like wearing girls' clothes but I don't believe they expected to see an erection on show."

He had to accept that he was going to be wearing female clothes for the day. Jackie tensed for a moment as a thought came to her mind. She told him to wait in the meeting room as she had something for him. She returned a couple of minutes later waving a pair of white cotton panties in her hand. "Don't tell anyone." I bought some panties the other day and had them in my desk drawer. Slip them on and they will give you some cover. That will make you feel more comfortable." Jackie squeezed her eyes together in a gentle smile.

How he could ever be comfortable in a mini-skirt working in an office full of women was beyond his comprehension. It was just degrees of humiliation. Wearing panties was one degree less humiliation than no panties.

"If I can help you with things like the panties, it would be great if you helped me too, Patty. I need this job. We can work together to make this easier. What do you say?"

Patrick took the panties and pulled them up and over his

erect penis. They stretched over the end and gave some cover and enabled him to pull his penis back below the skirt hem. "I guess so Jackie," he mumbled. He had little choice.

She tightened her grip on his hand. It felt warm and reassuring. How quickly the tables had turned. He was now reliant on this young inexperienced girl.

"Come on," she said. "Let's go and meet your new work colleagues and get to work." She pulled him into the main office and his head dipped in shame. His body burnt hot and nervous.

Chapter 10 — A short skirt and hairy legs

Giggles and comments behind hands greeted him when he moved around the office. He felt eyes following him. He told himself that they would get bored in time. The women would get used to a man in a short skirt. Eventually.

An unintended consequence of the cover story that Elizabeth had given about him being a transvestite helped. It meant they understood why he was wearing female clothing even if it didn't explain why the skirt was so short. They found it amusing.

He was grateful to Jackie for giving him the panties although his erection strained to remain inside the tiny cotton briefs. He manoeuvred his erect penis to one side to hold it in keeping it pushed back and above the short hem of the skirt. He hoped his wife or Ms Forrest didn't come back onto the floor and make him remove the panties. For some reason, they had not thought about covering his penis. Patrick struggled to understand what had happened to him in the past thirty minutes. His mind was a whirl of confusion and shock. He was dizzy and thought he might faint.

Jackie was his island of kindness in the ocean of vindictive women. She took him around the office holding his hand to introduce him to the ladies. He could not describe the emotions he was having at meeting women while dressed in a tiny pink pleated skirt and a tight pink blouse. He felt sick. A combination of abject ignominy and light-headed elation swooned in him. Around forty women worked on the 4th floor office; Jackie introduced him to each one, all the time her hand in his.

He felt like a complete fool in his little skirt with dark hairy legs and bare feet. Every introduction took him into a black pit of humiliation as they giggled and sniggered. He heard a couple of comments about his bum, the g-string of his panties showed the bottom part of his bum cheeks. Unless he bent over when it was fully exposed. He had never realised before how much women had to keep their legs together and bend from the knees to avoid giving a show.

His balls kept slipping out either side of the small panties, splitting them into two sacks. The little patch of cotton at the front struggled to cover his erect penis. He had to be careful as he moved and sat down. It was better than nothing. And he had a constant semi hard-on.

Jackie introduced him to everyone as Patty. She apologised to him gently but reminded him this was her instruction from Ms Remington. Every time she introduced him to another woman she mouthed an exaggerated silent 'sorry' to him. She was sweet. She was trying to help to make his experience less bad knowing he was embarrassed about the situation. He swallowed the remains of his pride.

The morning passed in a flurry of instructions from Jackie. She had positioned him at the workstation next to hers. The room was arranged in five rows of eight desk workstations. He was thankful that his row backed against a plain partition wall even so he felt the stares. Jackie had the corner desk and he had the next position o they were not in the open. On the other side was an older lady of around 50. She was unable to stop looking at him. He sat facing his screen, attempting to avoid eye contact with her. Or anyone. Jackie tapped in on the shoulder and made him jump.

The benefits of being tucked away in the corner were soon shown to be an illusion. Jackie smiled and mouthed, "Are you OK?"

He smiled back weakly and nodded.

"Be a dear and get me a notebook from the filing cabinet, Patty," asked Jackie sweetly.

His head dropped as his eyes glanced over to the cabinets on the other side of the room. His sense of some comfort at being out of sight of all but Jackie and the leering lady next to him was shattered. He would have to walk across the room just as things had calmed down and the ladies were getting on with their work.

"Please, Jackie, don't make me go over there. Everyone will look at me. Can't you go?" he pleaded.

She touched his arm with light fingertips. That smile again. His stomach turned over, she was cute. "You'll have to do it at some time, you may as well start. Yes, they'll look but they'll get used to how you look."

How long was that going to take, he thought? His eyes pleaded with her silently.

Her face hardened. "One more thing, Patty. Your wife told me that you have to address me as Ms Swann. You can't call me Jackie or we'll both get into trouble." Her lips parted to show a white set of neat perfect teeth.

There was nothing he could do. "Yes, Ms Swann." He got up. Faces around the room lifted.

Jackie returned to her screen. "Good girl," she said, her face impassive.

Did she just say, good girl? He waited a moment and watched her typing, oblivious to what she had said. It must have been an accident. He would let it pass this time. Jackie worked in a room full of women and it must have been a slip of the tongue. It had to be. She wouldn't have said that to him., she was too sweet.

He pushed his chair back as carefully as possible but immediately heads shot up across the room like a Mexican wave at a sports stadium. This was going to be difficult. The only thing to do was to get on with it. He padded over to the filing cabinets in the far corner of the room in his bare feet. Eyes front, avoid the stares, he told himself.

The cabinets were grey and business-like in cold metal with three large vertical drawers. A line of women sat at desks arranged at right angles to the other rows, their backs to the filing cabinets. He put on a casual air; inside he was burning up. The chatter of the room went quiet. Embarrassment burnt his face as he stood in front of the drawers. Forty sets of eyes burnt into his back.

He pulled out the top drawer where the files needed to be hung. The rollers echoed around the silent office floor. The notebooks were at the back. He stretched across on tiptoes. His tiny skirt rode up to expose his bottom cheeks.

"Cute bum," a voice rang out. He flipped his head around to look, his face an instant shade of purple redness. The room exploded into laughter, the silence broken as a rush of indignity filled him.

He pulled out the notebook in a panic while he tugged at the hem of his skirt in vain with the other hand. The skirt was too short to cover his bum cheeks. He planted his feet back on the floor still holding his skirt down with one hand. In his haste, he dropped the notebook. Jackie appeared at his side as if by magic.

"Calm down, Patty." She laid a hand on his arm. He was grateful she was there as support. He wasn't alone. "Don't worry, dearie," she said softly. "It was an accident. Pick the book up and then bring it over to me."

Jackie folded her arms as he knelt. He bent at the knees keeping them together, the skirt surrounded his thighs. His throat choked. He told himself not to cry. This morning he had been travelling to the office in a smart business suit and tie looking forward to being a Vice President. Now he was the most junior person and forced into a tiny skirt while picking up stationery from the floor watched by an office of leering women.

This was more than a trial. It was a bad nightmare. At the same time, he'd met the lovely kind Jackie. She was shy and genuine. If anyone had to see him in a skirt, he would have chosen it to be her.

She cared. She cared even though she was under

instructions from his witch of a wife. She had even found him some underwear to put on and saved him from a worse experience: walking around in a tiny skirt with his penis and balls exposed. He had Jackie to thank for avoiding that nightmare.

Anger flared inside him at what his wife had done. She could have made him suffer at home but she hadn't. She had humiliated him in front of an entire office of women. How could Elizabeth do this? Yes, she had discovered that he was being deceitful but they were both in the marriage to get something. In his case, he wanted some of her wealth. In her case, she'd wanted a toy boy to hang on her arm. Her vengeance was complete. His plan was now a failure.

He stomped back to his desk, head down, notebook clasped to his chest. His skirt flapped around the tops of his thighs. His legs looked slim and incongruous — hairy wasn't a great look with a mini-skirt. The chill of cool air lashed around his balls which were spilling out of the tiny panties.

He sloped back to his desk, avoiding eye contact with anyone in the room. He wanted to lock himself away, to avoid this ignominy. If he didn't look up, he could pretend no one was looking. He passed the notebook to Jackie as he sat back in his chair, his head down.

"Thank you, Patty. Good girl."

She'd said it again, it was no accident. Jackie was typing on her keyboard, her long red nails clattered on the keys. She furrowed her forehead in concentration. He had to say something. He was sure she hadn't meant it, she was just being thoughtless.

"Jackie?"

She looked up and raised her eyebrows. "Haven't we forgotten something, Patty?"

He had forgotten he had to call her Ms Swann. He grimaced. "I'm sorry, Ms Swann."

"Good girl. Don't forget next time. Now, what did you want?"

He flinched again. *Good girl.* Again."Ms Swann." He swallowed. "Please, my name is Pat or Patrick. Patty is a girl's name. And please don't call me a good girl."

The lady on the other side pretended to type but listened

with interest.

"Should I call you a bad girl then?" Jackie giggled at her joke. The older lady snorted, unable to contain her amusement.

He was distraught. He'd thought that Jackie was a single ray of kindness and now even she found him and his predicament amusing. The day crashed around him. A disaster. "No. Please don't call me a girl."

"I'm sorry, Patty, but it's not up to me. Elizabeth said I have to refer to you as a girl. I have no choice. She said you liked it, that's why you're a transvestite. Elizabeth said..."

"OK, OK, I get it." Patrick slumped in his chair. Elizabeth was grinding his self-esteem into the dirt. She was getting full revenge for his plans to take her money. At the same time, Elizabeth enjoyed him being feminine. Those trips to the hairdresser and nail bars were before she'd heard his indiscretion on the phone to Mike.

He had no other option for now but to get on with his work and put up with the clothes. The ladies would soon get bored with him in his little skirt. At the end of the day, he would get his male clothes back and he could go home and pack. He'd take his suitcase and leave. It would be the great escape. He had no money and nowhere to go but that was a better option than this. He needed his male clothes back.

But where were his clothes? Ms Forrest had left with them on her arm. She'd return them to him at the end of the day. He couldn't go home on the train dressed in a tiny pink skirt. Even Elizabeth wouldn't do that to him. Would she?

Chapter 11 — Vulnerable

This had been the worst day of his life. He watched the clock above the filing cabinets count down to 6 pm and still no sign of Elizabeth with his clothes. He had been stripped in the office and put into clothing more suitable for young girls. That had to be illegal under employment law. You can't force men to wear female clothes.

Whatever the vagaries of the law might be, Elizabeth had painted him into a corner. He didn't have any other source of income or a place to live. He had cancelled the rental contract on his apartment and signed that so-called contract for Elizabeth. He felt trapped. His best option was to allow her this day of revenge and hope things returned to some level of normality.

His original plan to get some of her money was not going to work now. The best he could hope for was to take her medicine for today and move on. Even Elizabeth wouldn't carry on doing what she had done to him today. It had to be a one-off to teach him a lesson. He had learnt that lesson.

The ladies in the office had left for the day. Most of them called out, "*Goodnight Patty,*" as they went, combined with giggles and excited chatter. The only consolation of the worst day of his life had been Jackie. She had shown him kindness and had given him some minor relief from the humiliation by finding him some underwear to wear. The thought of spending the day with his penis and balls barely covered made him shudder. He was unsure if that was with excitement or horror.

Jackie had also left for the evening. He had asked her to speak to Elizabeth to get his clothing back. She told him she couldn't as she was a junior worker and didn't have that kind of access to the CEO. He didn't know what to do. He was dressed in a pink skirt and blouse. Bare feet, bare legs. He was stuck at the office if he couldn't find his male clothes. He couldn't go anywhere until Elizabeth deigned to turn up.

A ping announced the arrival of the lift. He watched as the lift doors swiped open and his wife strode out like a hard gale followed by Charlotte, her executive assistant. Charlotte was like a mini version of Elizabeth. Younger and less elegant but similar in appearance and style. There was a faint similarity in them. He disliked how Charlotte hung on every word of Elizabeth's supposed wisdom. Like a pupil to the tutor.

Charlotte was carrying a pair of white flat ballet-style shoes. Where were his clothes? They approached him and Elizabeth spoke. "I can't let you go home dressed like that, Patty."

His body slumped in relief in his chair. Thank goodness. He could get back into proper clothing and escape from this hell. But where were his clothes?

"So," Elizabeth continued as Charlotte watched on with rapt attention. "I'm going to leave earlier than usual and you can come home with me in the car."

Charlotte passed him the ballet shoes and spoke in a similar tone to her mentor. "Put these on Patty."

"Where are my clothes?" he said.

Elizabeth sighed. "You have your clothes on, Patty, now come along. Put your shoes on and let's go."

She was going to make him suffer a little longer. At least he was getting a lift home. He slipped the ballet shoes on. They were better than being barefooted. Elizabeth's eyes darted to his crotch. "Are you wearing panties? Who said you could wear panties? Where did you get them from?"

He smeared his skirt down. He didn't want to tell her it had been Jackie who had given them to him. That would get her into trouble. His mind raced for an explanation.

Elizabeth tutted as he dithered. "I'm waiting for an answer." Elizabeth glared at him and lent forward.

"I found them in a drawer. They were new, in a packet. I don't know who they belonged to," he lied. A good reply he thought.

Elizabeth's expression told him that she didn't believe him. "I didn't say you could wear panties so take them off."

The two ladies crossed their arms as he delayed. He didn't want to remove his panties. He was in a fix. Elizabeth saw his hesitation and his reluctance.

"Take them off now and come with me or you'll make your own way home, it's your choice. I'm leaving right now." She marched back to the lifts, Charlotte in pursuit like a puppy. "I can't believe I was thinking of being so kind to Patty by taking her home," Elisabeth said to herself.

Charlotte shook her head as if to say she couldn't believe it either as she pressed the lift call button. He ripped off the panties from under his skirt and raced to the lift. She had check-mated him once again. Elizabeth glanced at the panties in his hand and shot a satisfied snort.

She pointed to a waste bin by the lift doors, "Put them in there, girly, you won't be needing them again. Your little clitty should be loose and hanging free. I want you vulnerable."

He tossed them away as she had ordered with an air of deep reluctance. He had no other strategy but to obey her; a pawn trapped by his queen. The lift arrived and the three of them got in. Elizabeth pressed the B for basement button. Patrick slid into the corner, concerned that someone else would get in later. The doors closed and he went down. They passed the third floor and he breathed in relief. He tensed again as they approached the next floor. They passed it and he allowed himself to relax. No one would get a lift from the first floor.

Ping. It jerked to a stop and the doors swiped open. Two young women entered, chatting to each other. One of them glanced at the button and saw the light around the B button. They continued their conversation. They had not registered him shrunken in the corner, engrossed in their discussion. They would not fail to see him once they got to the basement.

Ping, the lift jolted to a stop and the doors opened into the basement car park. The smell of petrol fumes and dampness greeted them on a damp breeze. He saw a small concrete basement with twenty tightly-spaced car spaces between square concrete pillars. Patrick remained in the corner of the lift.

The two young ladies stood politely to one side to let him, Elizabeth and Charlotte out first. One put her arm against the open doors. Elizabeth grabbed Patrick's arm and pulled him towards the open doors. They spotted him and their two mouths gaped open.

He gulped then went with his wife to her long sleek black car. It was parked in a bay with her name on a sign above it, screwed to the wall — *CEO Remington PLC, Elizabeth Remington.*

They got in and Elizabeth drove up the ramp, waited for

the automatic barrier to rise, and into the busy high street. He sat beside her in the passenger seat, his slim hairy legs peeking out from under the short pleated skirt. His bare bum cheeks and balls stuck to the leather seats. Elizabeth's face was set tight and annoyed. He stared down at the glove compartment in shame and humiliation. Charlotte sat in the back and chatted with Elizabeth.

He noted Elizabeth calling Charlotte 'Sis'. The name rolled around in his mind. Charlotte was Elizabeth's sister? His wife had never introduced Charlotte as her sister. How odd. That was the similarity then. But they were years apart in age, Elizabeth was old enough to be Charlotte's mother. He sat back, surprised. How many more secrets were there?

He heard Charlotte call Elizabeth 'Red'. He couldn't understand why Elizabeth was called Red; her hair was brown. They trundled through the slow London traffic, heading out to the west and his wife's home. His prison.

They got home after an hour of crawling in traffic. They entered the house and were met by Clara in the entrance hall. She showed no surprise to see Patrick dressed in pink girl's clothing. It was clear that Elizabeth had brought everyone into her game. Elizabeth told Patrick he should go to his room. "I suppose it's been a somewhat traumatic day for you. We'll be up in an hour or so with your instructions for the evening and tomorrow at work."

He swallowed hard and sloped upstairs to his room to find temporary refuge. He would take the opportunity to shower and change into his normal clothes. Male clothes. The drone of the three women murmuring in the kitchen faded as he made his way to his room; tiredness swept through his body. It had to be the stress of what Elisabeth had put him through at work. He pushed into his room and tore off the horrible blouse and jerked the skirt down to his ankles and stepped out of it. He grabbed a towel that Clara must have left for him on his single bed and went to have a shower. He'd wash the day away and start over.

He returned to his room, the towel wrapped around him. He felt a little better: refreshed. The day was now behind him like a bad dream. He sat on his bed and pushed back his long damp hair with both hands. He blew out slowly, happy that the day was over. It was behind him forever. It was finished and Elizabeth had her fun. He had been punished and utterly humiliated. He supposed, in her position, he would have done something nasty too. He wouldn't have thought of anything so unusual as a punishment. It was time to get back to real life now.

He went to his wardrobe and pulled open the door and stepped back. Strange small brightly coloured clothes hung from the rail. He stared for a moment in shock. He opened the mirrored door. The shelves were stacked with clothes; not with the socks, tee-shirts and underpants he'd left there that morning. In their place were packs of stockings and panties. He shot a look at the other side and his desperation mounted. Heat rose from his face as he saw skirts, dresses, blouses and cardigans hanging there. They were in yellows, pinks, whites and purples. This had gone beyond a joke.

A cough came from behind and he spun around. Elizabeth was leaning on the door-frame. She stepped into the room like an empress entering her servant's quarters. She swiped his towel away from around his waist. She stepped back and held it up, head on one side, taunting. He placed his hands over his penis.

"Elizabeth..."

"Downstairs. Five minutes. Don't make us come up to get you."

"I don't have anything to wear."

"Yes, you do, your wardrobe's full of pretty clothes. Put a nice dress on. You've wasted one minute so you're down to four minutes."

She left, her heeled footsteps stamping down the hallway. She was still annoyed with him; this woman bore a grudge. There was no way he was going to put a dress on and then go down in it for everyone to laugh at. He sat on the bed and put his elbows on his knees and cupped his chin in his hands. Think, he told himself. He had to have a plan. He needed to stop reacting to events controlled by Elizabeth and be proactive. He had to escape from his vengeance-filled wife.

He saw he had two problems. Firstly, he had to find something to put on that wasn't feminine. Secondly, he had to form an escape plan. He needed to find a way to flee from

Elizabeth's world. Problem number one was how to get through the evening without any more humiliation. An idea evolved in his mind. He decided to do everything his wife asked him to do. He could pretend he had accepted his feminisation and humiliation. He would pretend that he was enjoying it. That would confuse her and hopefully make this feminisation game less interesting for her. It might put her in a false sense of security. He could then make his escape.

He shouldn't make it too obvious. For tonight, he would play as if he were fighting against her feminisation. He wouldn't put a dress on to go downstairs, he'd find a towel to cover up. That would be a show of defiance to which he would then submit to a dress, apparently readily,. He had to pretend he accepted the situation.

He chuckled to himself, he was going to take back control. Her great intellect can only take her so far he considered. It was still possible to outsmart her.

The next problem was where to escape to. He had been an only son and his parents had passed away. His sometime friend, Mike? No that wasn't an option. Mike had three children, a fierce wife and a crowded family house. He wasn't on the best of terms with Mike's wife. She blamed him for leading Mike astray several times. Late nights drinking and she suspected some womanising. That wasn't going to work. Mike's wife would never allow him to stay there.

His aunt? His only family. That was it. His mother's sister, Melissa, was much younger than his late mother and she lived in London. He hadn't seen her lately but blood is thicker than water, isn't it? She was single and had a large house. This was the answer.

"Three minutes." Elizabeth's voice called up from below.

He would call his Aunt Melissa. She was twenty years older than him, around the same age as Elizabeth. He chuckled to himself realising that Melissa reminded him of Elizabeth. He had never thought of that before, but he hadn't thought about Aunt Melissa before now either. They hadn't kept in touch since his mother's funeral five years ago. She was family, it would be fine. It wouldn't matter that they hadn't spoken for five years, family blood ties would overcome that, they always did in the end. She wasn't the warmest lady in the world but that didn't matter, he needed a place to stay while he got back on his feet. He could then find a new job and a place to live and forget all about Elizabeth.

That's a plan, he thought to himself. He lay back on the bed feeling pleased with himself for the first time in several days.

Chapter 12 — Covering his little dignity

Elizabeth's voice came from below and brought him out of his temporary relief from the current reality. He got up, poked his head around the door and into the corridor. There was no one around. Giggles from the three women sounded from below, they were enjoying the evening together. He trod as silently as possible to the bathroom, still steamy from his earlier shower. He scanned the room. No towels.

"Two minutes." Elizabeth's voice floated up the stairs.

Heat rose through his body. He was panicking. Do what she wants, he told himself. Go down and find out what she wanted but remain covered in a towel to pretend he was fighting against her. But there were no towels. His eyes fell to the side of the white enamel sink. He spotted a hand towel. He swiped it up and pulled it around his waist. It was small.

"One minute." Elizabeth's voice boomed out around the house.

The towel covered his penis and balls but wouldn't wrap

fully around his waist. Half a leg was exposed and most of his hip. He glanced at the mirror above the sink. A strained face glared back at him. He had to hold onto the towel with one hand to avoid it falling off. He couldn't tuck it in. Never mind, this would do. He straightened up and admired his slim boyish physique and some confidence drained back. It was a good look with the tiny towel. A treat for the waiting ladies below he thought.

"Now, Patty."

"I'm coming, Elizabeth." He replied thinking that his wife did not need a megaphone, such was the strength of her voice.

He left the bathroom and padded to the stairs in bare feet. The sounds of laughter wafted from the kitchen. He heard chinking glasses. They were happy. He gripped the little towel tightly and descended the stairs. His right leg protruded from the small towel like a slit pencil skirt. A treat for the ladies he chuckled to himself. Be positive, they may be acting like dragons, but Elizabeth, Clara and Charlotte were also real beauties. A lightness swayed in his head as he considered his clever plan to get away from this hell.

He traipsed towards the kitchen. Hearing Elizabeth's deep voice so close produced a wary feeling. His newfound shard of confidence sunk as he approached the kitchen. He walked in, head down, cheeks flushing, a tight grip on the towel.

Their conversation ceased. The three ladies sat in a huddle around a kitchen island. A black granite work surface glistened under soft LED spotlights. White gloss wall and floor units lined two sides of the room. Clara looked up. She had an almost drained wine glass in her hand. Charlotte watched without emotion, waiting for a lead from her mentor and sister. Elizabeth glared, it was as if steam was blowing out of her ears. He froze. His confidence evaporated like a drop of water in the desert sun.

Elizabeth was still in her business wear – a dark blue knee-length business skirt and jacket. She put her wine glass down on the work surface with a loud clunk.

"How dare you call me, Elizabeth." She glared, unblinking.

Clara's lips quivered, suppressing a laugh. She was enjoying this. What was wrong with calling her Elizabeth at home?

Elizabeth continued. "I told you earlier at work that you will call me Ms Remington. Ma'am is a good alternative."

Her glare bore into him. He averted her look, staring at the white wall for help. It was as cold and uncaring as Elizabeth.

"I thought that was something for the office," he mumbled. He wanted to curl up. He re-tightened his hand on the towel.

Charlotte stepped up to his face. "Say sorry, Ms Remington."

"How can I call my wife, Ms Remington? That's ridiculous." His plan was unfurling like a flag in a hurricane.

Slap. Charlotte's hand stung his face.

He spluttered. He fought to control himself in the shock. Charlotte had slapped him. He flinched his arm ready to return the slap. He held himself in time. He reminded himself, he had to play along with their game. Lull them into a false sense of security. The plan was crumbling a little. e told himself not to rebel, hold firm. It's not too late to recover, he thought.

He breathed in, let them think they had won. He counted silently to five. Do it, he told himself. "Sorry, Ms Remington."

His eyes fell to the cold floor.

"That's better, girl." Elizabeth's glare dug into him.

Clara finished the last drops from her wine glass. Silence, the swish of a passing car sounded from the road outside, the sound of tyres on surface rainwater splashed through the room. He waited. Something else was coming.

Elizabeth shook her head slowly from side to side. "I told you to put on a pretty dress not come here in a stupid little towel. Take it off."

He turned to go back upstairs. If he had to put a dress on then he would grit his teeth and do it for tonight. He had to play at being submissive and humble. He had shown his rebellious side, now it was time to play the beaten man.

"Where are you going?" Elizabeth's eyes glared like headlights. He was the rabbit in their path.

He stopped at the doorway. "To put a dress on. Ma'am."

"Are you stupid? Take that towel off now, here. Besides, you have a task to do and you'll need to be naked for that. In some ways, it's worked out for the best," Elizabeth said.

He did not want to remove his cover despite his attempt to

pretend to be submissive He held on to the towel. It was whipped away. Charlotte had it in her hand. He was naked. Clara leant forward, both elbows on the granite surface, watching events like he was a one-man West-End London theatre show. Elizabeth's face crinkled into satisfaction, her anger salved by his latest humiliation. She was winning. She loved to win.

He cringed in the doorway, naked and exposed in front of the three ladies. He locked his knees together like a knock-kneed child. He felt humiliation on top of indignity mixed with ignominy as Elizabeth wandered around him. She eyed him up and down like a predator contemplating its next meal. He shuddered. It was difficult maintaining his resolve to do as she wanted. His hands slid over his penis. She pulled them away.

"The problem is, Patty my girl..." She walked, circling him. Her heels clipped on the tiled floor. *Clop, clip, clop clip.* He hunched as she looked down at him. "If you're going to wear pretty little dresses and skirts then you need to lose your hairy body. Don't you? Body hair doesn't work on a girl, I'm sure you'd agree. How can you be pretty with all that nasty body hair?"

He didn't understand where this was going. She kept bringing in new tactics, it was difficult to keep up with her. Charlotte wandered away and returned with a small white plastic device with a lead and plug. He looked at her and back to Elizabeth. Charlotte held out a hand. She had a small electric shaver in her palm. The metallic end glinted in the spotlights.

"Take the nice female electric shaver, plug it in and remove all your body hair. From neck to toes. You can do it there on the floor while we finish our wine. Good girls don't have hairy bodies do they, Patty? And you're going to become a pretty girl, aren't you?"

He snatched the shaver from Clara's hand like a truculent schoolboy.

"Don't forget to shave your cute little clitty and pussy balls. But…" Elizabeth took a small sip from her wine glass. She made him hang before she finished her sentence.

He shook with anger at his vulnerability. One naked man and three strong women who were dressed. He sat on the floor in the silence of their stares. He liked being the centre of attention but not like this.

Elizabeth continued. "Leave the pubic hair above your little clitty in a cute triangle shape. It's overgrown. It needs to look pretty and feminine."

The three women moved back to the kitchen island and Clara topped up their glasses from a second bottle of wine. He sat with his back against the wall holding the electric shaver, one hand over his genitals. They had all seen them but it was a natural reaction to cover his privacy. He was not so private now. He had to play at compliance. Shaving his body hair was not the end of the world, it would grow again. His compliance acting was tougher than he'd expected.

He turned the electric razor on, the buzz vibrated through his fingers like an annoying bluebottle. He shaved his feet then legs and then chest. He lifted his arms and did under his arms. Finally, he shaved off the hair from his arms. The ladies lost interest and chatted amongst themselves. Once finished, he ran a hand over his newly smooth legs. They looked odd and felt lighter. It was a nice sensation. He had let his hand drop from his penis and balls. He was lost in thought and heard sniggering. The women had been watching him rubbing his legs.

"Someone likes her new smooth look," Clara said. This raised a further bout of giggles. It was unusual to see Elizabeth laughing. She was relaxed, the old Elizabeth, the one he knew before she had turned on him. Or, more likely, the new Elisabeth who was winning and in total control.

He had left the hair above his penis as Elizabeth had instructed. Elizabeth went to him and knelt by him. She ran her hand over his chest. He smelled the wine on her warm breath, the musky odour of her perfume. She looked over his smooth body approvingly, eyes glistening with pleasure. It was as if she had a new power flowing from his body into hers. She lifted his smooth balls and nodded. Then she tutted at the sight of his pubic hair.

"It's a little too wide and untidy." She traced it with a fingernail. His flaccid penis was stung into action and grew. Elizabeth raised her eyebrows.

Charlotte went to them. "I'll do it, Red. You get on with

that work you needed to do."

"You don't mind, Sis?"

"No, not at all."

They were discussing his most private of parts as if he wasn't there. Elizabeth handed over his erection to her sister with two fingers. "Here you go take this then. You know what I want?"

Charlotte nodded and pulled Patrick by his erect penis out of the kitchen and up to the bathroom. She was rough, tugging him upstairs with force, the skin stretched out at the base of his erection like a small sail. Her hard grip on his erection was also stimulating, it was as if someone had set fire to his body. He had never experienced someone treating his penis so coldly and roughly, without tenderness. For some reason, it felt good. It was incredible. This was surprising. He was not about to tell her he was enjoying her rough grip.

In the bathroom, Charlotte bent over and fished about in the cabinet below the sink. She wore a mid-thigh flared skirt with a large red-rose pattern. He caught a glimpse of a stocking top and a flash of a thong disappearing into a rounded bum. His erection throbbed. She found a can of gel and a hand razor. She knelt in front of his erection. The breath from her nostrils breathed against the exposed red head of his erect penis, like the breeze from a butterfly's wings.

Her lips were no more than an inch away. Plum-red lipstick on her plump wide lips set firmly together in concentration. He willed her lips to open and move forward onto his desperate penis. It was as hard as he had ever known. Her breath wafted around it again, a cold breeze of gentle air swum down on his sensitive desperate cock. It stood out stiff like a parched bone.

He wanted her to chew on his erection, he wanted to feel her tongue and teeth against his retracted foreskin. Her mouth moved closer, a twitch and they would touch his slit, expanded at the end of the most intense erection ever.

She gripped his penis sideways and away from her full lips and perfect white teeth. A wave of pure disappointment washed against him, the hint of possible ecstasy receded like an ebbing tide.

She sprayed the shaving gel around his pubic hair. It was

business for her. She pulled the hand razor down the side of his pubic hair. She shaved and rinsed the razor under a running tap, shaved and rinsed. He closed his eyes. This was so erotic, why hadn't he thought of this before? He had found plenty of girls willing to sleep with him in the past but it had been a quick blow job or a bang and then finish. This was something else, an erotic teasing. She wiped water over his pubic area and around his balls and cock. He put his head back. He wanted to cum, This was incredible. She finished.

"Let's show Red," she chirped and pulled on his aching cock guiding him downstairs to the kitchen. He hadn't yet looked at what she had done, so caught up in the sensation of the moment.

Charlotte pulled him into the kitchen and let go of his penis. He was disappointed that her hard uncaring touch had gone.

"Ta-dah," announced Charlotte, her hands pointed directly to his small neat triangle of pubic hair sitting half an inch above his firm penis. The point of the triangle pointed at his depilated member like an arrowhead of humiliation.

Laughter greeted her announcement. "Perfect," said Elizabeth.

He looked down at it. His eyes went wide at the sight of his pubic hair. Charlotte moved in front of him and looked as if she were deep in thought. She pushed hard on his erection, placing it between his legs. She pulled his legs together to trap it between his bare thighs and stood back. The ladies squealed and clapped. He closed his eyes for a short moment then opened them and stared down.

He looked like a girl: smooth slim legs and his penis hidden between them. All that remained was the neat triangle of a feminine-like pubic mound.

Chapter 13 — Smooth & feminine

He woke with a jump from a jab to his shoulder. A sharp nail dug into his skin. The room was dark, chilly. He shook his head, a finger jabbed him again. Then a woman's voice told him to get up. It was like a dream. If it was a dream, then Clara was in it. His covers flew away. A flash of cold air hit his hairless, naked skin. A shadow moved across him and the side lamp flicked on. He awoke with a start. It was Clara and it wasn't a dream. The bedroom clock clicked onto 05:02. Five am!

Clara was standing above him. He couldn't focus, his eyes were blurry with sleep. He struggled to wake fully despite the freshness of the morning air on his body. The warmth from the radiator by his bed was beginning to break into the room.

"Get up if you want to go to the office by car this morning," Clara barked.

He rubbed his eyes, still closed. "It's 5 am," he moaned, not yet sure where he was.

"Elizabeth gets to work early. You can either go with her by car or travel by train. In a pretty dress."

He opened his eyes opened instantly. He was at his wife's home in his new bedroom. Naked and hairless. Clara was looking at something down on the bed. He gazed down and was horrified to see his penis pointing erect and firm at the ceiling.

"What's the story, morning glory?" Clara smirked. "Thinking about the pretty clothing you'll be wearing today?"

He was awake and alert instantly. Yesterday's events flew through his mind on fast forward. He sat up sharply. Clara was going through his wardrobe. She looked fresh and bright as if she had been awake for some time. She pulled out a hanger. A white dress hung by its shoulder straps, flared from a high waist into a short skirt.

"Come on, Clara, you can't be serious. You want me to wear a white dress?"

"No, *I* don't." Clara's face was impassive as she let her response hang in the chilly air. "*Elizabeth* wants you to wear a pretty dress to work today. The ladies there will be so excited to see your nice smooth legs. Now get dressed, showered and be downstairs in fifteen minutes. And I'm Mistress Clara to you, Patricia."

Clara threw the dress over his erection and stomped out as he was about to complain about being called Patricia. This was going too far. Patricia? He had thought that Patty was no more than a childish diminutive of Pat. Now Clara was calling him by a girl's name. He considered his next move. He had to take the initiative. He didn't want to go to the office again, especially in a short dress.

The offending dress lay across him. It was white with short sleeves and a mini-skirted part. He threw it back on the bed and went to get showered to think about how to deal with Elizabeth's plans for the day.

After shaving and showering, he returned to his room, his erection still strong. He smiled to himself. Despite her humiliation, his testosterone was high. He was a real man and putting him in female clothing would never change that. He admired his erection and stroked it softly. The white dress on his bed shuddered into view, reminding him of Elizabeth's plans for the day. His erection strengthened seeing the dress. That was odd, he thought.

"Slip the dress on, there's a good girl. There's no time to play with your little winkie now." He hadn't heard Elizabeth behind him.

"Please. Enough. You got your revenge, can't this finish now?" he pleaded.

Elizabeth sighed, she had no interest in a discussion. "Put the dress on, Patricia, I don't have all day. It's simple. I'm offering you the choice of travelling in a dress in the car or travelling to work on public transport. Your choice. It's one or the other."

He hated what she was doing to him. Her revenge had gone beyond what was acceptable. She was being vindictive now. He had a third choice; refuse to go to the office. That choice meant dismissal and meant he would be out of her life. He would also be out of her home and without money. He had to go along with her latest outrageous demand until he escaped to Aunt Melissa's.

He shrugged. The women at the office had all seen him

yesterday in a skirt, so this was no different. He'd pretend to go along with Elizabeth's demands as he'd planned. At the office, he'd phone Aunt Melissa and plead with her to help him. Use the family connection. Melissa would help him, he was sure. Family. That was the plan and today he would call her. She'd help him and this was ending today.

He looked up at his stunning-looking wife and a pang of longing and attraction confused him. He hated her and desired her at the same time. There was something deeply erotic and exciting about her dominance over him. That was impossible to understand. He was an alpha man, not a sissy. For a moment he felt free at the thought of being a sissy. No more need for him to take charge or be the leader. He could sit back and let Elizabeth take responsibility. That felt horrible and enticing at the same time.

He was in an early-morning state of bewildered helplessness. He pulled the dress over his head and tugged it down. It hugged him perfectly. His erection strained as the soft material glided over his skin and against the exposed head of his penis. The material was fine and delicate and floated gently around his bum and the tops of his thighs. It tickled against the end of his erection. He felt that familiar tingle from his balls and along his shaft. No! Don't cum, he told himself. Not now, not with his wife watching. His tormentor. But it felt so erotic, so liberating. Elizabeth, the dress, the material. The situation. He twisted his face. Hold it in he ordered himself, don't ejaculate.

"What's up, Patty? She looked at him intently. "Are you in pain?"

He shook his head and tightened his mental fight against cumming. The thin material of the dress moved against the head of his erection as he fidgeted. The thin slit at the end of his erection was sensitive and he was on the edge.

Elizabeth registered what was happening; pleasure formed in her eyes. "Oh, you love the dress. Excellent."

He pulled the material away from his erection. His penis swung in the air, better this than cumming. Elizabeth remained, fascinated and intrigued by his internal battle. Her eyes pivoted onto the end of his penis and focussed in like a pair of binoculars. "How marvellous, Patty. I can see pre-cum.

Don't tell me you don't love the dress, I can see you do."

Horror. A drip of pre-cum was indeed hanging from his swollen slit at the end of his erection. Elizabeth twisted towards the corridor and she called out. "Clara, you have to see this."

Desperation hit him. She had called Clara to watch. The hem of the dress hung lightly over his erection, stark white over a reddened shaft, like the sail of a yacht against a mast. Clara shot into the room and, for a short moment, she looked puzzled. Then the shock at the sight of Patrick struggling.

"He's about to cum in excitement." Elizabeth stood out of the path of the imminent ejaculation, moving Clara gently to one side. It was too much. Euphoria welled in his head and warmth grew in his stomach. It extended down into his erection. The inside of his balls swelled and bubbled like a witch's cauldron. Then, an explosion of ecstasy and release. His cum shot into the room like a flame of white-grey fluid. Elizabeth and Clara flinched back involuntarily. It splatted onto the carpet and landed into a puddle. A tiny moment of heaven and release. Then instant mortification. He had ejaculated in front of Elizabeth and Clara. The shame of being excited by wearing a dress.

Elizabeth stomped to him and held up the hem of his dress as the final rivulets of his cum leaked out. "We need to keep your mess off your pretty dress, Patty. We don't want tell-tale signs on it for the office do we?" she said with a hint of humour in her voice.

He had expected his wife to be annoyed but she seemed satisfied with what had happened. Clara wandered out and returned with a sachet of wet wipes. She bent down and wiped his limp cock clean. She pulled back his foreskin and wiped around the head. He was surprised and confused. They were being nice to him, within the circumstances of his predicament.

Elizabeth added. "That will be the last time you cum for a while so I hope you enjoyed that."

He nodded in abject shame. He didn't understand what she meant. He wasn't expecting sex with her for a while, that much was clear. Masturbation was always his fall-back option. Elizabeth was unable to stop that, he thought with a shard of anger.

Once Clara had cleaned him up, he followed Elizabeth and Clara downstairs. Over breakfast, he worried. He was wearing a tiny white dress with bare legs, arms and feet. It was October and cold outside, especially at this time of the day. Even running to the car outside would be freezing in what he had on. Or rather what he didn't have on. He sat at the breakfast bar while Elizabeth and Clara chatted, ignoring him. His bum and balls stuck to the leather of the stall. Clara disappeared from the room.

Elizabeth looked up at him and hunched her shoulders and grinned in what seemed a friendly manner. She was happy, or at least satisfied. He returned a watery smile to her. Clara came back into the kitchen with arms full of plastic store bags. She tipped them out onto the work surface. A pink quilted jacket, packets of stockings, a bright pink cardigan and white women's court shoes with a thin one-inch heel.

Elizabeth rubbed her hands together. "Put these on, Patty. They will keep you warm."

So he wasn't to freeze, they had thought of him. A little. He stood and pulled on the cardigan, buttoning it up in a surly manner. He had no choice. He was going to have to wear a dress to the office and be humiliated again. But warm and humiliated was better than cold and humiliated.

Clara undid a packet of tan hold-up stockings. He stared at them with horror. A darker tan elasticated frill ran around the top.

"Slip these on, Patricia, they will keep your legs warm."

His anger returned. This was getting ridiculous. He stamped a bare foot. "No." He had forgotten to be compliant. Immediately he regretted it, it might derail his escape plans.

Clara and Elizabeth looked a moment then both laughed. "Suit yourself. Patty. You're the one who'll be cold. You're going to be spending the day in a little white dress so what is the difference if you put on stockings too?" Clara said smugly.

He needed to recover the situation and resume his compliance. "I'm sorry, Ms Clara."

He took them from her and pulled the sheer stockings onto each leg. They glided on smoothly. Like the dress material, it was a feeling he had never before experienced against his skin: sexy, erotic.

Clara placed the shoes on the ground. He slid his feet into them. Immediately, he was slightly taller and had the feeling of leaning forward. The tautness in the back of his calves was not unpleasant, as if he had run uphill. For a short moment, he put himself inside a woman's mind. He understood the feelings they had. He shook the thoughts away, they wouldn't help him.

"Let's go, Patty. Put your jacket on." Elizabeth swung her car keys on one finger, like a gunslinger spinning a revolver.

Patrick put on the pink padded jacket she offered him. It finished on his waist; six inches of white dress peeked out and flared out from the bottom of the coat. His long stocking-covered legs shone in the kitchen lights, the elasticated tops exposed. For a moment he swooned at the incredible feelings. He shook his head. He had to fight this, it wasn't right.

He walked from the kitchen into the hall. A streetlight peered in through the frosted glass of the front door. The sun had yet to rise. He told himself it was unlikely anyone would be about.

"Hold on, Patty." It was Clara. "One more thing that Elizabeth wants. To keep you under control."

What did she mean? Clara faced him and put her hands around his neck. Her cheek was close to his. Sweet-scented perfume and soap. She pulled on a strap against his windpipe. Tight but not restrictive. His fingers went up to feel it. It was a leather belt. He heard a click. What was this? Clara moved back, her scent lingered for a moment then faded.

He peered in the mirror hanging on the hall wall. It was a pink leather dog collar; small fake diamonds glistened. A metal ring hung loosely from it. A small chrome padlock in the shape of a heart was clipped to the fastener and sat against his neck.

He glared at Clara. "What's this? What have you done?"

Clara held up a thin chrome chain. A pink leather loop at one end matched the collar wrapped around his neck. She took the metal end and clipped it onto the metal link on his collar, and tugged. He put his fingers in the collar and felt around it.

"What?" was all he could manage while Clara held the lead out and led him towards the front door. Her hand was tucked inside the leather loop. She waited as if it were the most normal thing in the world.

"Elizabeth wants you under control. She thought it best to keep you on a leash, like a naughty pet."

His mouth moved but no words came out. Elizabeth glided into the hall wrapped up in a black fleece coat with an imitation fur-lined collar. Clara passed her the leather loop and opened the front door for her. Elizabeth tugged on the leash and the dog collar dug into the back of his neck. The cool air rushed in like water pouring into a sinking boat.

Elizabeth tugged Patrick to the open door. He was framed in the doorway. The street, bathed in amber light from the street lamps, was fifteen feet away from the front door. A fox's eyes glinted in the front garden and it stood like a statue for a moment, staring. A mangy tail hanging limply between its legs. It shot away. Nothing else was around. Elizabeth and Clara kissed each other on both cheeks.

Elizabeth stepped outside, pulling him with her by the lead. He stepped out after her and into the fresh morning air. A breeze blew hard against his flimsy dress and pushed it onto his penis, shaping the front like a small tent. Elizabeth breathed in, seemingly oblivious. She pointed her key at the car and it bleeped twice and flashed its lights. She moved off the step towards the car, leash in hand, pulling him behind her like a pet.

Chapter 14 — Escape plans

The cold air bit against his face and genitals. He was thankful it was still dark. A damp chill rose from the grass of the front garden and up his dress. It swirled around his bare smooth penis and balls.

The amber light from the street lights didn't reach the driveway where Elizabeth's sleek dark sports saloon waited in the drive. His short jacket gave him warmth for his upper body, his lower half quickly got cold. He wrapped his arms around his body and trotted towards the car behind Elizabeth. The chain of his leash hung loose. He dithered a moment and Elizabeth gave two jerks to pull him along towards the car. Its windows were covered in dew.

Elizabeth tucked the leash loop around her wrist and opened her car door. She rummaged around on the door shelf and retrieved a scraper with a rubber end. "Be a good girl and take this and clean the windows before we set off."

He took the scraper, bemused. Elizabeth stood by him

while he wiped the windows around the car. She held the leash as they went around the car. The cold air around his penis and balls was uncomfortable now and they had shrunk. The occasional car passed by, but no one was walking this morning.

Elizabeth let go of his leash and they got into the car. Elizabeth told him to drive. Once in the passenger seat, she took his leash again and wrapped it around her wrist. He pulled out of the drive and into the street to make the slow drive across town from west to east London.

He drive to her office and stopped the car in the small underground concrete car park under the building. A second day of mass humiliation awaited him. He got out of the car and his dress rode up, exposing his shrunken penis and balls. He scanned the area in a panic. There was nobody around.

Elizabeth took his leash again, tugging gently to move him out of the driver seat. He shook his head. What was she up to? Surely she wasn't going to walk into the office pulling him on the lead.

No one entered the lift as they rode to the 4th floor from the basement. Elizabeth stepped into the open-plan office, the leash loose in her hand. He followed, not that he had any option as she tugged him in by the lead. It was 8:30 and some of the women were already at their desks.

Elizabeth strode to his desk as he followed behind. Jackie sat at her desk, it was tidy and organised. A mobile phone and a keyboard were the only items on the surface. She glanced up and her face took a moment to register the sight of Patrick in a short white dress and a leash in Elizabeth's hand.

"Jackie." Elizabeth's face was serious and firm. "I don't want you to give Patricia any panties today. She's not allowed to wear them." She waited.

Jackie's face flushed, worry etched on her forehead. "I'm very sorry, Ms Remington, I thought I was helping. He… she was feeling uncomfortable… I…"

Elizabeth's face softened. "No harm done, Jackie. Now take her leash. I'm handing her over to you now. Ensure she behaves. If she wants to go to the toilet, I want you to go with her taking her by her leash. You'll need to make sure she sits down like a good girl."

Elizabeth had not mentioned this before. Was Jackie supposed to take him to the toilet like a child?

Jackie's face flushed again. "You want me to take Patty to the toilet when she needs to go?"

"Yes, and she has to leave the door open so you can see she's sitting down. She needs a lot of training and how you cope with that is important for your development, Jackie."

Patrick's mouth dropped open and then Jackie's mouth mirrored his. Elizabeth handed the leather lead to Jackie and strode off. Jackie and Patrick stared at each other for a minute. Unblinking. Then Jackie recovered her sunny composure and her eyes ran up and down his body.

"That's a pretty dress, Patty."

He looked to the floor. Jackie let the lead drop by his side and she unclipped it. She ran her hand down his leg. "Nice stockings, do you like them?"

"No, Ms Swann."

Jackie had brightened up, recovering swiftly from the surprise Elizabeth had delivered. She was a person who took unexpected changes in her stride, a sunny and kind disposition he thought. "Well, never mind Patty, I'm sure you'll grow to love them."

"I hope not to be wearing these clothes for that long," he grumbled.

His thoughts turned to how to contact his Aunt Melissa. He didn't have her phone number. He knew she lived in Hampstead, north London. He was sure he could find the number online.

His bladder ached after the long drive into the office; he would hold out as long as possible. He turned on the PC and googled the name, 'Melissa Stone'. A long list of women appeared with images and Facebook links. None were his aunt. He clicked on more images and his screen filled with thumbnail photos of women of all ages. Blond, dark, long-haired short-haired, old, young and in the middle. He didn't think there would have been so many women called Melissa Stone.

He scrolled through the list. He found her: Melissa Stone, lawyer. That was her, long auburn hair and strong face. She had the usual business side-on photo, half body, sitting down.

Plain grey background.

He clicked on the image. It took him to a LinkedIn page. He read through her professional profile. It covered her legal practice, qualifications, office address and website. There was a business phone number. He would try later if other options didn't work out. It was risky, a secretary would probably answer it and possibly shield Melissa from his call. He decided to send her a message on LinkedIn.

> *Hello Melissa, how are you?*
> *This is Patrick your nephew.*
> *It looks as if your business is going well.*
> *I know we lost contact but I desperately need help and you're the only family I have. I got married recently but it's not working out well. Could I come and stay for a couple of weeks until I can*

work things out? I have loads of skills and I will get myself back on my feet again very quickly. I'll try not to be a burden on you.

Please help me, my marriage has turned into a nightmare and I'm desperate. I'd love to come to stay with you today. Please

Love from your nephew, Patrick.

He pressed send and sat back. A wave of relief washed through him at taking action. Then the doubt. Would she respond? If so when? He remained logged in to LinkedIn and minimised the browser. He stared at the blank screen. A tap on his shoulder made him jump. It was Jackie.

"Be a dearie and make me a coffee, Patty. And ask the others if they would like one too."

His shoulders dropped in shame. The three other ladies in the row had heard her and all nodded. His immediate problem was that he needed to pee. He leant over to Jackie. She looked at him askance as his face got closer.

"Ms Swann, I need to go to the toilet."

She jumped up. "Come on, Patty, let's take you to the ladies' and then you can make the coffee for everyone." She clipped on his leash.

He cringed in humiliation. He followed her out of the room and into the corridor and the stairs. Jackie pushed purposefully on the ladies' room door and held it for Patrick. She pulled him up to an empty cubicle by the lead and held the door open for him. His head went down he went into the cubicle and sat down, his dress flowing around his thighs. The lead hung by his side. Jackie's hand remained on the door, holding it open. He struggled to go with her watching but it was Elizabeth's order and Jackie wasn't going to disobey the CEO. The door to the room opened and another lady walked in and then stopped seeing Patrick sitting on the toilet and Jackie holding the door open.

The lady stared. Jackie explained, "Ah", and then they both giggled conspiratorially. Elizabeth had briefed everyone about her 'transvestite husband who wanted to be treated as a girl'.

He finished peeing and endured Jackie reminding him not to forget to clean his little thing with a piece of toilet roll. "We don't want drips on the floor do we, Patty?"

He dabbed at the end of it with the tissue and stood, pulling his dress down as far as possible to cover his penis and balls. Jackie unclipped his leash and told him to go to the kitchen to make the drinks. He went to the deserted kitchen area, relieved no one else was there. The kitchen had a sink and cupboards and a common area with a table for eight and a sofa. There was a kettle and microwave oven on the work surface and a line of wall cupboards above a white ceramic sink.

He delayed as long as possible in the kitchen, getting some peace from his humiliation. When he could delay no further, he placed the drinks on a tray and walked steadily back to the main office, dropping off the coffee mugs on each desk. He sat at his desk and waited for Jackie to immerse herself again in her work.

He opened the minimised LinkedIn page: no reply yet to his pleading message. Melissa was obviously busy, too busy to be checking her social media sites every few minutes. His initial excitement at his plan began to waver. What if she didn't answer him today? He couldn't bear another day and evening being humiliated by his wife Elizabeth.

Chapter 15 — Kitchen humiliation

Patrick plodded through to lunchtime on a variety of minor tasks for Jackie. Time moved like slow-motion lava flowing from an eruption in a disaster movie. At midday, Jackie asked Patrick if he would like to go out for lunch with her and a couple of her female friends from the office. It was a sweet offer but he declined as politely as he could. He had no intention of leaving the building to walk around in broad daylight on a busy high street while wearing a short dress. Even with his newly shaved legs, kitten-heeled female shoes and stockings, he would look ridiculous.

He wandered to the kitchen after Jackie had left, conscious of the eyes of the office ladies following him. He felt the familiar effect in his penis at the odd excitement of his humiliation. His penis hardened under the dress and he fought against it, his face screwing in concentration. Even semi-hard, it would poke below the short hem. He didn't want that.

Two young ladies sat at the table in the kitchen area. They stopped chatting as he entered. He had hoped that the area would be empty. Both women were in their mid-twenties, one blond, the other brown-haired. Both had the fashionable Princess Kate long, waving hairstyle. Their short, brightly coloured skirts were nothing like their idol's style. The blond girl's short red pencil skirt had ridden up as she sat, exposing her long but thick shapely legs. The brown-haired girl's mid-thigh skirt was pastel yellow and gathered in soft box pleats. Her legs were slim and she wore high wedge sandals.

They sniggered as soon as they spotted him. Their eyes were not on him, they were looking at something lower. He glanced down. The tip of his penis showed below the hem. He had a semi-erection and it was causing them great amusement. He was mortified and tugged the hem over it which caused more giggles.

"Do you like wearing a dress?" the dark girl asked between her giggles, which seemed forced, he thought. Large loop earrings showed through her thick brown hair.

"It looks to me like he loves wearing dresses, Sophie," the

blond girl replied and they collapsed into exaggerated laughter once again. She fidgeted on her chair to keep her panties covered in the small tight skirt. Why did some girls choose to wear such short skirts and then look uncomfortable as they attempted to stay covered? He knew from the experience of the past two days, it was uncomfortable.

Sophie stopped laughing as quickly as she had started. "Come over here." She indicated with a nod of her head that he should approach them. "We're only joking, being friendly. Join us, all girls together." She looked serious for a few moments. Her expression was too staged.

Maybe they were being friendly? He would like friends here. Other than Jackie, he had never felt so alone, so humiliated. He wandered over to the two girls, his eyes falling over their bare legs and short skirts. Blood coursed into his penis, exposing more of the shaft from beneath the hem. The girls' eyes followed it. He pulled hard on his dress, a losing game.

The girls exploded into fits of laughter again. He supposed he would have done the same the other way round, it didn't mean they were being nasty, it was natural. A man in a dress that was far too short with no underwear is not a normal sight in a working office.

The darker girl reached out and ran her long red fingernails from the hem of his dress and down his smooth thigh. "You have very smooth legs. Do you like being a girl?" She looked up at him through black false eyelashes, the faked innocence was mingled with a sparkle in her eyes. She continued to run her nails up and down, getting closer to his erection with each run. Up and down her finger went.

His penis shot to full hardness as the back of her hand grazed against his balls and then hit against his hard erect penis.

"You haven't answered me. Do you like being a girl?

"No," he said with a catch in his throat. His penis reaction called out his lie. He should move away but their attention and her hand drew him in like a magnet.

Sophie suddenly lifted his dress exposing him fully. Her nails scratched along the length of his penis, electricity rushed from his toes to his scalp.

"You like being a girl." Her eyes flitted to her friend and back to his.

Annie moved in closer. "He has a little pubic triangle. How cute, how feminine."

She traced it out with a fingernail. He wanted to pull away, he should have pushed her hand away. The delicate scratching of her nails along his shaft was playing havoc with his senses and he needed to cum. Their attention on his penis and balls was too exciting for him to stop them. He wanted to but at the same time, he didn't. Annie touched his balls with her thumb and forefinger. She rubbed them together, squeezing slightly.

"Your balls are so smooth." She moved her mouth towards the end of his erection, a hairsbreadth away. Her red thick lips pursed and she blew on the end of it with a puff. He groaned. She moved her mouth away and they giggled again. She moved her lips back in, almost touching the end of his firm penis again.

She pulled his foreskin back fully. He gasped as his full red engorged penis head was completely exposed to the fresh cool office air. He should pull away. Run. What if someone came in?

But, it felt incredible. Two young women, paying attention to his penis and balls while he was in a beautiful short dress with fine soft material. He wanted to cum, it would only take a little effort, a small rub. Her finger ran over the end of his penis and rubbed on the slit at the end. Her mouth opened and hovered over the end.

"Would you like me to suck it?" Her breath was light against his erection.

"Yes, yes. Please." He was desperate. His eyes closed, shutting out the location, experiencing only the sensations, the intense wonder of his emotions. She only had to put those lips over the end and he'd shoot into her mouth. He needed that touch, that warmth and dampness of her saliva. He opened his eyes. Her mouth opened over the end. She withdrew a little. He shut his eyes again. Any moment he'd feel her tongue, her thick lips on his penis head.

"Then tell me you like being a girl."

"What?" He opened his eyes and shuddered with frustration. He wanted to shout at her to do it. That wouldn't work. They were in control, not him. They were using his desperation. She moved her wide-open mouth back over the end of his erection, not quite touching, open, teasing. Her warm breath sent shivers over him. The darker girl watched intently.

"Tell me you like being a girl. I can't do anything until you answer me."

He was so desperate it hurt. His erection was so hard it ached. "Yes, yes, yes. I like being a girl." They were controlling him using the desperation to cum swirling inside him.

Annie leant back in her chair and folded her arms. "Good. I thought you did."

"What?" he said. "I thought you were going to suck me." A single gossamer touch against his penis and he'd shoot cum everywhere. One touch, that's all it needed.

Annie moved towards him. "I prefer men and you said you liked being a girl. So I can't suck a girl, can I?"

The two girls erupted into fits of childish laughter. They touched each other's arms. He stood, his erection throbbing and pre-cum dripping. He wanted to run, cum and disappear all at once. An instant change from the love of being exposed and feminised to utter embarrassment.

How could he have been so stupid? He felt as if his face were melting. Don't cry, he told himself. He wanted to change into trousers, to be a man again. What had seemed exciting when his sexual needs were so elevated, was now sordid. Tears welled in the corners of his eyes. He walked backwards away from them. His back hit the kitchen cupboards, his erection waving and throbbing.

"Oh dear, I'm sorry darling. We were only playing we didn't mean to upset you. We thought you liked wearing a little dress. That's what Elizabeth Remington told us before you arrived. And that we could play with you." Sophie looked concerned. Annie stopped giggling. Her face was now sympathetic.

"Come over here, darling. Come on." Sophie held her arms out to him.

Kindness after the taunting. He guessed they knew they had pushed it too far and realised their mistake. He walked back to where they were seated at the table. Sophie flung her arms around his waist from her seated position. His erection poked into her chest and she pushed it away and resumed the hug as if it were an annoying fly.

Annie eyed his erection and spoke without taking her eyes away. "Don't you like wearing a dress then? I think he does Sophie." Her gaze drifted to the dark-haired girl.

"No." A sob entered his faltering voice.

"Then why are you so hard?"

He shook his head. He didn't know, he didn't understand it.

"Would you like to cum?" Annie was running her fingernails along his erection again.

Were they playing with him again? His desperation won out against his pride. "Yes, I need to cum. I'm desperate." Honesty blurted out before he could think straight.

Sophie moved away and looked directly at his erection. "Then you should. But I have an idea. We would like to know if you can hit a target with your cum." Annie nodded and said "Yes."

Sophie looked back into his eyes. "You can masturbate yourself."

"What? In front of you two. In the kitchen area? At work?"

He gasped. Desperate as he was, this was something else. He wanted them to suck him, to touch him. Masturbation was a poor alternative to what he had expected, for what he needed. Touching himself while these two young ladies watched was too much.

"Before you start, we had a bet earlier about how long your erection would be. I said six inches, but Annie thinks seven. I have a tape measure in my bag and we want to measure it."

He looked around and over his shoulder. Annie touched his arm. "Don't worry most people are out for lunch and the others are having lunch at their desks. No one will see. It'll be between us."

He felt included in their secrecy. He was making new friends. Maybe. If he went along with their childish behaviour, what was there to lose? For the humiliation and embarrassment, at least he had some attention. They had already humiliated him completely and they had already seen his erection in all its glory. He may as well let them. He was defeated. He shrugged.

Sophie produced a tape measure from her handbag and

placed it along the length of his erect shaft as Annie held his dress up. The touch of her fingers under his penis sent a spike of ecstasy into his stomach. That sensation of imminent discharge appeared again. The girls looked closely at the tape measure, touching their heads as they inspected it. "Six and a half inches. We both win," announced Sophie. They laughed.

He put his face in his hands. A tap on his erection made him look up. It was Sophie. She was holding a piece of printer paper. She had drawn a circular target in red lipstick, three concentric rings with a single bullseye. She held it away from her and the table. "See if you can hit the bull's eye."

He moved back. "Oh come on, this isn't a game. This is my dignity."

This caused more giggles from the two girls. "Your dignity flew away a long time ago. Now go. Shoot at the target." Sophie rattled the paper. "Rub yourself. Come on. Let's see if you can hit the target."

He was unable to move. His erection pointed directly at the paper target three feet away at the same level. Sophie shook the paper to jog him into action calling, "Come on, come on." She laughed at the double meaning.

Annie moved up to him and kneeled beside him facing the same way. She grabbed his erection in one hand. She moved her red-nailed hand up and down it. He watched the top of her blond head. He was so desperate to cum, he didn't push her away. She closed one eye and put her head alongside his shaft, as if aiming his erection like a rifle at the target while making ricochet sounds. He closed his eyes and allowed her to run her soft hand up and down.

The feeling of imminent release tingled at the end of his cock and then suddenly he burst out hitting the bottom of the paper target. More cum dripped from his deflating erection. He breathed in deeply, eyes closed. Dreaminess floated over him.

"You missed. Failure," called out Sophie.

"What's going on?" A woman's voice. It wasn't Sophie or Annie.

He opened his eyes in alarm. Ms Forrest stood in the kitchen entrance, one hand on her slim boyish hip, a piece of paper in the other hand.

He pulled his dress over his penis. The two girls stammered and then closed their mouths. They looked shocked. He wanted to curl up in a corner under a blanket.

Ms Forrest was livid. "You two." A single finger pointing at them. "Back to your desks. Patricia clear up your mess now. Disgusting."

Sophie and Annie raced out of the kitchen, stifled giggles followed them. Patrick went to the sink in a horror-filled daze and looked in the cupboard under it. A cloth and cleaning spray were there. He took them and wiped over the floor, cleaning up his cum. He picked up the paper target, his cum stained the bottom area below the girls' humiliating target. His face flushed and blotches of red ran across his cheek and neck. How had he let himself be taken along such a degrading route? He screwed up the target and put it in the bin under the sink. Ms Forrest's steady unwavering glare bore down on him.

"Patricia, go back to your desk. I'll deal with your misbehaviour later. I can't believe it, performing sexual acts in the staff kitchen. Disgraceful, not to mention unhygienic. Elizabeth will hear about this."

Chapter 16 — Makeup time

He ran back to his desk, hands holding down the hem of his dress. This has to end, he thought. His moment of release and satisfaction was destroyed by Ms Forrest. It had been a debasing episode in the kitchen with Sophie and Annie. An awful experience that had, at the same time, been exhilarating. He had never had a sexual experience with two women before. Maybe it was a stretch to say it was a proper sexual experience, but the attention they had given him, or more precisely how they had played with his penis was an exhilarating new experience.

He sat at his desk and checked his LinkedIn account; the memories of Annie and Sophie's humiliation gave him warm feelings. Aunt Melissa had not replied yet. It was probably too much to expect. He had to bite the bullet and call her office. He looked for Melissa's office number on her page. He found it and picked up his desk phone. A mature lady's voice answered after one ring.

"Hello Melissa Stone's office, Joanne speaking." The deep voice was almost masculine sounding.

He gave his name as Patrick Ashleigh and asked for Melissa. He told Joanne he was her nephew. The lady asked him to hold while she checked. He heard a click on the line. A wave of tension in his body.

"Sorry, Mr Ashleigh, but Melissa is in court all day today. She's then going straight home. She's not returning to the office today. Why don't you meet her at her home tonight? If you're her nephew, I'm sure she would mind. I'll send her a text to let her know you want to speak to her."

He asked for Melissa's mobile phone number but Joanne refused to give it. "I don't know that you're her nephew so I can't do that. Go to see her and I'm sure she'll be happy to see you if what you say is true."

He said he might do that. He thanked the receptionist and hung up. He didn't want to spend another evening at Elizabeth's house. The thought of another day in the office was too much to bear. He had to find a way to get to Melissa's home in his current clothing.

An idea came to him at that instant. He would make himself look more feminine and make the journey to Melissa's home on public transport. It might work. It was London and people were more used to diversity than other UK cities and towns. Even if someone did notice him as a man in a dress, it was unlikely that anyone would bother him. It would be uncomfortable. It was worth the embarrassment of one public transport journey in a dress to get this nightmare over with.

He was sure Jackie would help him look more female. He had no intention of telling her why, of course. She had to believe he had accepted his fate. She was a little naive and he could use this trait.

As he waited for her to return from lunch, he rummaged in her desk drawers. He found what he wanted. She had left her public transport travelcard in the drawer. He took it out. He felt bad but he had no money or credit cards on him. He had stolen from her but she wasn't stuck there, she could use her credit card to get home. She wouldn't be stranded. It wasn't stealing, it was borrowing. He'd pay her back once he got straight. Maybe he would come back one day and take her for a drink? She was lovely, that would be nice. However, his need was greater than hers. The plan was now clear. He slipped Jackie's Public Transport Travelcard into his desk drawer and closed it shut.

Five minutes later, Jackie returned, saying hello as she sat down. She looked excited. She was bursting to say something. It blurted out in a long stream. "I bumped into Sophie." His heart missed several beats. "She told me all about what happened in the kitchen. Patty, you are such a naughty girl. I would never have thought you would do that. In the kitchen." She tapped him on the arm.

He was distraught. Now the whole office would know what happened. He said nothing and pretended to look unconcerned. Focus, he told himself. His mind swung to his escape plan; he prayed she wouldn't look in her drawer and notice her Travelcard was missing. It was time to put the second part of his escape plan into action. To look more like a woman and enough not to attract too much attention. No time to waste he'd ask her before she got too busy.

"Ms Swann, could you do something for me, please?"

She looked up with a sweet smile. "Of course, Patricia, you naughty girl. I hope you don't want me to play with your little tinky like Sophie." She giggled. She wasn't going to let the story drop.

"If I have to wear female clothing, then I may as well go all the way. I want you to make up my face like a woman's. Please?"

Jackie looked surprised for a moment then her face melted. "That's a great idea. Let's do it now." She parked the kitchen incident, this new development overtaking her thoughts.

This was the reaction he had hoped for. Jackie groped around in her handbag and withdrew a small pink rectangular bag with a zip across the top. She told him to close his eyes and that she would make him up. She rolled her chair towards him, enthusiasm was written across her face. She told him this would look good for her with Ms Remington and Ms Forrest. It would do her no harm at all to make Patty look more feminised.

He closed his eyes and smelt her sweet perfume close in on him. Her soft makeup brushes whisked against his eyes and face. He felt lipstick drawn across his lips. His eyelashes tickled as she put on mascara. Her fingers worked through his hair. It was over his ears and flowed down his neck. Jackie fluffed it up with her fingertips. She pulled on his swept-back hair and brushed it over his forehead. It tingled against his eyebrows. A clip and a weight appeared on his earlobes. His hands shot up to feel dangling metal. Earrings.

"Open your eyes, Patty." Jackie cooed.

He flicked them open with difficulty. They were heavy and sticky. The office had gathered silently around as Jackie had worked on his face. She thrust a mirror in his face. Shock. He looked like a woman. Faintly pretty although there was something masculine in his facial profile. The clip-on earrings dangled and danced from his ears. This would do. If anyone looked hard it was obvious he was a man. But this was London, most people would not even look. He swallowed hard. He was as ready as he would ever be.

"Thank you so much, Ms Swann." He forced an artificial happiness into his voice.

Jackie clapped and the office ladies surrounding them

joined her. A round of applause. "I'm so happy you've decided to go along with Elizabeth's plan. It makes it so much easier. It's for the best, Patty."

He had a moment of guilt. He had tricked her, his only friend there. But needs must and his needs were greater than hers. With the makeup, he might get away with it. The earrings were a bonus. He didn't want to wait any more. He was going to leave the office now and go straight to his aunt Melissa's home and wait for her, even if he had to wait hours. He wanted to escape from this hell Elizabeth had brought on him. It was time to enact the second part of his escape plan.

Chapter 17 — Runaway

He got up from his desk as Jackie went back to working on her computer screen, deep in concentration. He told her he was going for a wander to stretch his legs and try out his new make-up around the office. Jackie looked up for a moment, pleased. Look casual, he told himself. His hand ran around his dog collar. There was nothing he could do; it was locked on. He pulled the little heart-shaped padlock around to the back of his neck so it hung down hidden behind his hair. The dog collar showed. He hoped it looked like a fashion accessory.

He went to the corridor to use the stairs, grabbing his pink coat on the way out. Using the lift would attract attention. It would look suspicious. He stepped down the stairs and to the ground floor, his small heels clicking on the tiles. He passed through the security barriers and walked fast to the exit door. The receptionist paid him no attention. He put his head down, the makeup was good. He knew he had a male physique and a masculine face shape. Not to mention his male walking style.

He pushed through the revolving door and into the street. Terror hit him. It was a bright autumn afternoon, a fresh breeze gusted and the watery sun was low in a vivid blue sky. There were people everywhere. His stomach turned over. He was in the street in a pink jacket, a short white dress protruding below it, clear stockings on his slim legs and shoes with little heels. He was dressed as a woman.

The fear of discovery hit him. He couldn't move. People rushed past, they were annoyed as he stood stone-still in the middle of the pavement. He needed to get moving to avoid attracting attention. He strode along the high street towards the train station. His penis rocked side to side under the dress. It was vaguely apparent within the fold of his short flared dress. No one was looking. Yet.

Melissa had then made it big in the legal field and had moved into a six-bedroom home in Hampstead. He entered the Overground train station on the corner of the high street; it nestled under a Victorian red-brick railway bridge. The modern orange London Overground train logo clashed with the classic architecture of a bygone age.

A train squealed to a halt above him and the piercing metallic sound of brake pads on wheels sheared through the air. He was attracting some looks from males which he guessed were for the shortness of his dress and his slim legs. They looked good. He approached the ticket barriers and tapped Jackie's card on the reader. It swung open. He was on his way to freedom. He clumped up the steps to the platform holding his dress between his legs. Anyone below would have got an eyeful of his barely hidden masculinity beneath the dress.

He waited on the platform, hands holding his tiny dress down. The breeze of an approaching train whistled and swirled and would lift the dress if he wasn't careful. Two men passed him carrying tool bags, plaster and dust on their clothing. Their mustard-coloured dirty boots were unlaced. Their eyes were glued to his smooth stockinged legs. He shuddered with cold and horror at being ogled by men. He supposed it was better they looked there than at his face. Yet, something was scintillating about being admired. He had great legs, why did he have to hide them before?

The train arrived and the more prosaic thought of not being spotted as a man reared in his mind again. The train doors slid open and he stumbled on. He found a seat and pulled his knees together, tucking the tiny hem of his dress between his thighs. The seats lined either side of the carriage and were sparsely occupied. The cold had shrunk his penis and balls and for once he was thankful for this.

The next obstacle was the change of trains which would take him on to the Hampstead line. Stations passed and his change station arrived. He jumped off and strode up the steps and through the station to find the Hampstead line platform. He kept his head low, his hands around his dress hem.

He saw the sign for the Hampstead line in the far corner of the station. Laughter and catcalls sounded from behind him. He swivelled around. Three twenty-something men were pointing and calling to him. He felt his bottom. The dress had blown up and his flat bottom exposed. He moved away quickly as the cat-calls rang out, telling him to stay there, that he had a cute bum. Did he give a good blow job?

He stumbled down the next flight of steps, his hands

holding his dress down as he balanced on his small heels. The Hampstead train was already pulling in. He felt a huge relief; her kept his head down and the earrings jangled against his neck.

He got on the train. Panic. All the seats were taken. He had to stand. It was difficult to hide now. Eyes flicked over him. Two middle-aged women stared at him from a seat. One nudged the other with an elbow then indicated his crotch area with her head. He had been spotted as an imposter. There was no option but to brave it out. This was London and people were likely to stare and comment but he probably wouldn't be bothered. Whispers around him hissed.

The train pulled into Hampstead Heath station as the looks and stares rolled over him. He stepped off the train, strode across the platform and through the hall and out of the station. He stood in the street, the vehicles crawled along and people milled around. Melissa's home was a fifteen-minute hike away. There was no other option but to stride out.

His feet and calves now hurt. His feet were unaccustomed to the angle of his foot and the narrower toe of the shoes.

Blisters had formed on his toes. He had to ignore them. He walked as fast as possible. A vehicle horn sounded from the road, a driver leered at him like a reptile. He shuddered. He was all legs and pink jacket.

He turned off the high street onto a quieter street. Three-story Victorian and Edwardian houses lined either side of the road like soldiers forming a guard of dishonour for him. The first spots of rain hit his head and the clouds were darkened overhead. The weather had changed. Another five minutes to his Auntie Melissa's house.

The rain grew in intensity and his hair became flattened. He turned into the road where Melissa's house stood. The wind drove into his face, he was worried his make-up might wash away. He was close now as he trudged along the road, his feet complaining. The rain soaked the unprotected part of his dress and it wrapped around his penis and bum like kitchen cling film. He was cold and miserable. The outline of his small cold penis showed. The dress became transparent in the wet. He prayed someone was home so he could wait inside for his aunt.

He arrived at the gate of his aunt's house. He hesitated as the rain hammered on his head and the pavement around him. The brick-built house loomed wide and high, detached with a small grassed front lawn. A six-foot-high green-waxy-leafed rhododendron bush was in the centre of the lawn, the buds closed for winter. Two medium-sized trees had lost their leaves and looked like skeletons praying for summer. Sash windows lined the ground and first floors of the house. A faint light flowed out from the ground-floor windows. Someone seemed to be at the back of the house.

He couldn't get any wetter now as raindrops dripped down his collar and his back. His dress was sucked onto his body and his hair was plastered to his forehead.

He swung open the garden gate and scampered to the front door. The house rose in front of him, imposing and grand. He stood onto a red doorstep and cowered beneath a small tiled porch. There was a circular brass doorbell on the wall. It was surrounded by a wider brass plate. He breathed in and pressed. A chiming tone echoed in the hall beyond the immense front door.

He waited. Nothing. His finger hovered over the bell push again. Then, he heard the faint swing of a door hinge from the depths of the house. He heard rapid approaching flat-footed steps, small and urgent. His hands moved to cover the front of his transparent, soaked dress. A shadow loomed behind the glazed black door. The metallic sound of the twist of a handle met his ears. The door opened, six inches, restricted by a thick golden-coloured chain at neck height. A single eye and cheek glared through the gap.

"Yes." The partial face of a short slim girl in her twenties met his. Her fair hair was pulled back tightly in a straight ponytail. There was a hint of Eastern Europe in her voice.

"Hello, my name is Patrick. I've come to see my Aunt Melissa." He wiped the raindrops from his face with one hand while he kept the other across the wet dress to hide his penis. He spotted diluted black mascara streaked across the back of his hand.

The young lady looked him up and down. "She not here. Come back later."

Chapter 18 — Refuge

She went to close the door on him.

This was going to be tough. "I'm Melissa's nephew. I need to see her. I can wait for her. Inside."

The impassive face stared out from the light and warmth. "She be late. I not know you."

"That's fine." He replied. "I can wait. Inside."

"She not say anyone was to come to see her."

"I'm her nephew."

"I not know that. And why you wearing a dress? You man."

"Call her, please? I'm cold and wet." He didn't want to discuss that particular problem with a housekeeper.

"Wait for moment," she said and closed the door.

He stomped his feet on the porch. Wet, miserable, cold. Five minutes passed. The chain slid smoothly behind the door and it opened. Fully. He stepped in. The young housekeeper closed the door behind him. Warmth enveloped and surrounded him. A cloud of steam rose from his back as he shivered. She stood still, her arms folded. "I text Melissa. She say OK, you can wait."

He guessed she meant text*ed* but wasn't about to give her an English lesson on the past tense. He was too cold.

"She say she know you her nephew and you wait for her inside house. She get message from her office that you come and Link-ed-in message. Have shower get changed into dry clothes. She home at 9."

"Thank you." He said. "What's your name?"

"Maja. Follow me to shower room." She was unfriendly, disinterested. It was as if he was interrupting her routine.

He kicked off his shoes gratefully at the front door, his feet were sore and throbbing. He shivered. A large liquid-filled blister sat on the big toe of each foot He hung his pink coat on an old-fashioned coat rack by the door.

She led him up a wide set of stairs to the first floor. She had an upright walk and didn't say a word. At the top of the stairs, a long landing led to a bathroom at the end. He followed her in.

Maja looked him up and down, a faint look of disgust on her face. "Wait. I get fresh towel." She strutted out of the bathroom, ponytail swinging.

A double-width shower extended along the far wall, a glass sliding door open and inviting. His feet warmed on the black tiled floor. Underfloor heating. He pulled off his soaked stockings and waited for her to return with the towel. He pulled at the hem of his dress without thinking, conscious of its shortness. His hair was flat on his head, wet and cold. He pulled off his earrings and laid them on the side. She returned and passed him an immense white towel. It smelt warm, cotton fresh and laundered. He hung it on a hook on the wall. The young housekeeper laid a bright green floor towel by the shower door.

He said, "Thank you."

She looked him up and down. "Why you wear dress? You lady-boy?"

"No, it's a long story."

She mumbled something unintelligible under her breath, looked him up and down again and left. He heard her stomp down the stairs in her flat plain sensible shoes. Strange girl, he thought. It didn't matter, he was safe and warm. When the chips are down you can always lean on your family, even when you haven't seen them for years. A warm glow settled over him and he felt sleepy with relief. He closed the bathroom door, removed his dress and turned on the shower. He threw the dress in a corner and glared at it in hate. That's the end of that episode he thought. Freedom. Escape.

He stepped into the shower and washed his cares and humiliations away in the hot soft shower of refreshing water. It rained down on his head and body. The cold washed away. He soaked for a few minutes and then turned off the shower. He slid open the glass door and stepped out onto the green floor towel. He moved to grab the large white bath towel from where he had hung it. He froze.

The housekeeper was standing in the open doorway. She lifted up a gown. "A robe for you. We no have men's clothing here. Only woman." She thought for a moment. "I guess that better for you, lady-boy."

He grabbed the towel and pulled it over his genitals. "What are you doing in here?" A fit of anger blew through him. He pushed it away. He needed Melissa and didn't want to annoy her housekeeper.

She didn't react, her face passive. "I am providing gown for you. I help you. Take, lady-boy."

He calmed down. She was an odd one. He took the gown with one hand and held the towel with the other. "Thank you. You can go now."

"Put gown on and you wait for your aunt in living room. She be surprised to see you, that is for certain. Lady-boy for nephew."

She left and he watched as she descended the stairs without turning back.

He dried himself and pulled on the gown. He sighed. It was mid-thigh length, a fine silk-like material. White with pink and green Chinese-style flowers over it. A woman's gown. He hadn't thought about that. His aunt didn't have a husband or partner so why would she have any male clothing in the house? Maybe she could send her housekeeper out tomorrow to get some trousers, tee-shirts and male shoes. There was to be no escape yet from the torture of female clothing but at least he was free of Elizabeth's control.

He went downstairs and into the living area. He heard Maja banging in the room behind this one. It must be the kitchen. One wall of the living room was lined with books in a teak-wood bookcase. A wide sofa rested along the other wall. The room faced the road through an enormous bay window. Patrick wandered over to the bookcase, the feeling of the gown was familiar against his thighs, soft and clinging like a dress. He was comfortable that it was longer than the dress Elizabeth had put him in. The one he had left in a damp ball in the corner of the bathroom.

He perused Melissa's extensive rows of books. Many were legal books. He spotted a novel laying on the shelf, a bookmark protruded from the pages. That was unusual as the rest of the books were neat, arranged alphabetically by the author's name. He picked it up. *The Cleft* by Doris Lessing. He moved over to another shelf. There were several novels by an author called Lady Alexa, *Becoming Joanne* and *A Sissy Cuckold Husband*. Odd. He guessed she must be an English aristocrat doing some writing on the side.

He went back to the Doris Lessing novel and took it over to

the sofa and flicked through it to kill time. It was a fantasy novel about a female-only society. He read the first few pages.

The rain lashed against the bay window. Inside the room was warm and cosy despite its size. The sofa was padded and comfortable. He sank into it as the past couple of days' stresses and bad memories seeped away. His eyes became heavy, his head nodded onto his chest. His lids closed and the book tipped away from his light grasp. He fell into a deep sleep.

Chapter 19 — Auntie's home

He dreamt he was hiding in a secret room. He was naked and people were looking for him. As he hid alone in the room, he had a strong feeling of being observed. But no one was in the room. He moved position, waking up, feeling sleepy. The feeling of being watched was so strong. He awoke with a start. His eyes were sticky from make-up and sleep. He wiped at and then dug at the corners with a fingernail. His gown had fallen open and he had an erection. The dream had been exciting.

A dream woman was standing in front of him, hands by her side, a black leather handbag in one. His sleepy eyes travelled from his erection to her black high-heeled stilettos with black stockings on long muscular legs. A pencil skirt sat above small smooth knees.

His eyes rose to see a matching fitted jacket bursting with a huge breast encased an even tighter blouse beneath. Thick auburn hair flowed around her face and over her shoulders like a wild waterfall. He shook his head. Was he still having a dream? If so, it was a dream with a fantasy woman. He focussed on her face. She was like a fifties movie star. He rubbed his eyes. Aunt Melissa?

"Auntie," he said, pulling his gown over his erection.

"Less of the Auntie, Patrick." She sat on the sofa, a discrete distance away at the far end. She crossed her legs, making her muscles look more formidable. For a moment he imagined being crushed between them. "And I'd rather you put your penis away." She stared. "Anyway, to what do I owe the pleasure after all these years." The tone indicated it was not so much of a pleasure but more of an imposition.

He noted the less-than-warm welcome. "It's a long story, Melissa."

"Less of the Melissa, it suggests we are close which isn't the case, is it? I haven't seen you for years." She seemed to be analysing him. "So. Why don't you start by telling me what's going on?"

He felt vulnerable at her lack of friendliness and that he'd been sleeping with an erection poking out. He recounted the story of his recent life with Elizabeth. He covered meeting her through to his escape from her office building. He missed out on some of the more intimate events that had occurred. Melissa listened impassively. No indication on her face of what she thought of his story.

Once he had finished after fifteen minutes of monologue, he waited for Melissa's response.

"That's quite a story, Patrick. It seems your wife might have some justification for her behaviour. Feminising a man by putting him in overly female clothing is a recognised and valid technique for their punishment and control. Petticoat punishment. I am fully aware of it as a process for improving male behaviour; men can be so boorish at times. Your wife sounds an interesting lady." She looked him over for a few moments. "So Patrick. What exactly do you want from me?"

Patrick shivered at hearing her comments and a sense of being made to feel like a naughty child enveloped him. He had forgotten his aunt had such an aloof manner and she was making him decidedly uncomfortable. She was his only option though so he swallowed his discomfort.

"Could I stay a while please, Melissa? I will stay out of your way and keep everything clean. Until I get back on my feet. Please?"

Melissa stood and, for a moment, he thought he was going to be thrown out such was the disdain on her face. "I haven't heard from you for five years. Since the funeral of my dear sister. And suddenly you turn up on my doorstep, in a dress, asking to stay with me?" She let out a deep breath. She contemplated something and sighed. "I suppose so. Take the bedroom upstairs at the front of the house. The one with the pink wallpaper. I'll ask Maja to find some clothing for you. You can't go around in that gown all day and night. You never know what might pop out when you're dozing."

Relief swept over him. He could stay with her although he saw she was less than enthusiastic about it. He had no choice but to put up with her disdain. Melissa called out to Maja. She scampered in, her face set on miserable. He thought this might be the time to ask if she had some way to remove his dog collar.

"No." Came Melissa's blunt response. He waited for an explanation. None came. She looked at Maja. "Be a dear, Maja, and find Patrick some clothing to fit him. He looks to be the same size as our previous guest."

Maja scurried out of the room.

He put his hands together in a praying fashion. "Thank you so much, Melissa, I'll make it up to you. Anything."

She looked down her nose at him. "I don't need anything from you, just do whatever I tell you and stop calling me Melissa. You can call me Ms Stone."

This was odd. "But you're my auntie," he complained.

"Unfortunately, yes, but Melissa is too familiar. We drifted apart, the family broke up. Ms Stone will be more suitable, it will keep this formal. It's how I'd prefer things."

He was confused. She was weird but he did not want to push things. She clearly didn't want him there so he would do as she said. "OK, *Ms Stone*." He exaggerated her name to make a point.

Maja scurried back in with a pile of clothing over one arm. She placed it on the sofa next to him and stood back. Melissa thanked her and she left in a hurry. Patrick thanked Melissa for the clothing and picked up the top garment. His eyebrows knitted in confusion. It was a grey box-pleated skirt, more like a schoolgirl's clothing than something for a man. He scrabbled through the other clothing. Skirts, blouses female tops. He stared up at Melissa.

"These are all female clothing, Ms Stone."

"I don't have any male clothing, why would I? Put those on, there's nothing else."

"But I've just escaped from all this feminisation nonsense. Can't you send Maja out to the shops to get me some male clothes? Please."

Melissa bent down to within six inches of his face. He smelt coffee, wine and a beautiful scent. "Patrick, I just told you I have no male clothes. There are no men here, only females. You can wear these until you can get your own clothing back."

He contemplated his options. There were none. Melissa stood to indicate the debate was over. "You may join me for dinner at 9 pm in the dining room. Be in the skirt and blouse. It's dinner, not a sleepover."

She stared a moment then left. He heard her high heels clipping up the stairs. He had merely swapped one aggressive lady for another. And he was back in female clothing. It was as if his destiny were following him around like a desperate pet dog.

Melissa had been an imposing remote auntie when he was younger but, on balance, she was the better option if he compared her with Elizabeth. He supposed she was being fair. Why would she have male clothing?

He pulled on the skirt. It sat three or four inches above his knee. At least it was better than the micro-skirts Elizabeth had put him in. Be positive, he told himself, this was an improvement in his situation. He was still in skirts but at least they were less revealing. Aunt Melissa was lending him the only clothing she had; he should be grateful. Despite that, he had a deep worry. This was not going as expected. A sense of foreboding ran through his body.

Chapter 20 — Surprise surprise

He wandered into the dining room at 9 pm as Melissa had told him. He was starving., he hadn't eaten a thing since breakfast. The room had high ceilings and a large wooden dining table dominated the space. The room was on the other side of the corridor from the living room and had an identical large bay window looking out to the front. A gusting wind whistled through the stark bare trees in the front garden. Inside it was warm and cosy.

Melissa hadn't arrived yet. He looked at himself in the wide wall mirror sitting above a low wooden wall unit. He wore the grey box-pleated skirt with a brilliant white blouse and black hold-up stockings. He had chosen the white blouse as he thought it may look a little like a shirt but the shaped appearance gave a female shape. His long hair lay on his shoulders, straight and smooth. The ends had curled up. He pushed his fringe back from his forehead.

Melissa breezed in at that moment. She had changed out of

her business wear and into a dress. He tried to avoid gawking at her. He didn't want to leer at his aunt but she looked incredible.

"You look much better, Patrick. How do you feel in the pretty clothes? Nice?"

Pretty? The word stabbed into his chest. It was a question of wearing the only clothing available. He didn't want to annoy her so he said, "They are fine thank you, Ms Stone." Using such a formal tone with his aunt stuck in his throat. He had to follow her unusual instructions if he was to be allowed to stay there. There was no other option.

She frowned and looked. "I asked if you felt pretty in them. Not whether they were fine."

He cleared his throat. That was strange. He had to reply. "Yes, I feel pretty. Thank you, Ms Stone." He swallowed hard. This was uncomfortable.

"Excellent," she replied, her face looking pleased for the first time since he had turned up.

He waited for her to sit. She took the head of the table and he sat to her left.

"Patrick, I have another guest for dinner. We'll need to wait a few minutes. She texted me to say she has been held up in heavy traffic."

Patrick stood up in alarm. "Guest? They can't see me like this. I'll have dinner upstairs. In my room."

Melissa was not perturbed. "Sit down, Patrick. You'll have dinner with us. I'm sure she won't be the least bit bothered by seeing you in female clothing. She's a dear friend of mine." She sat closer to the table. "Anyhow, you feel pretty, as you told me, so I don't see a problem, do you?"

He bit on his bottom lip. "No, Ms Stone." He remembered his aunt's instructions. Apprehension swam back into his body. This was weird.

"Who is it? Who's coming?" He stammered.

"Don't worry about that, you can sit there looking pretty when she arrives." Melissa chortled at what she said."

"But did you warn her I would be here and I had to wear female clothing?

She ignored him. That meant no, he guessed. They sat in silence for a few minutes. Then the doorbell rang out, echoing to a stop. Patrick's stomach turned. His skin fluttered. Another humiliation awaited. He thought he had escaped from this and now it had returned in another guise. Less threatening and vengeful, but it was as if he were caught in a loop where all roads led back to feminisation. It wasn't as bad as what Elizabeth had put him through. He clung to that thought.

He heard Maja's footsteps going to the front door. It creaked open and the muffled voice of a woman greeted Maja. He heard Maja's voice. "Please to put coat on rack. Madam, Melissa is waiting for you."

There was some more mumbled conversation, undecipherable from the dining room. The hard sounds of stiletto heels sounded on the wooden floorboards of the hall. He imagined the visitor hanging her coat up. More mumbled speech.

"Please to come this way, Madam." Maja's sounded voice again, higher than the murmur of the deeper-voiced visitor.

Shoe heels marched down the entrance hall purposefully, *clip-clop, clip-clop, clip-clop.* Sharp and hard. The dining room door swung open. It was Maja. "Please Madam Melissa, your guest has to use bathroom after long time in car. Bad traffic she say, too long journey."

Melissa nodded a thank you as the stiletto heels clipped further down the hallway. A door whined open then clicked shut. "I bring starters, Madam Melissa," Maja said and Melissa nodded in agreement.

Patrick's stomach grumbled. He wasn't looking forward to Melissa's guest seeing him. At least it wouldn't be worse than what he had gone through earlier in the office kitchen. At least he was properly covered and he supposed even a grey schoolgirl-style skirt was better than a tiny white dress. He had found a pair of clean white knickers in his bedroom so he was even covered up down below.

His mind swung to the events of the two young ladies humiliating and playing with him. Sophie and Annie had used his ejaculation for target practice. He had never experienced such devastating indignity. He had never had such as powerful orgasm either. These were strange new feelings. Horrible and wonderful at the same time. He smoothed the skirt over his thighs as they waited in silence for the guest.

The distant sound of a toilet being flushed reached his ears. His stomach turned and butterflies fluttered inside. Come on, he told himself, this cannot be worse than what Sophie and Annie had put him through. Be strong. Brave it out.

A door opened in the hall. Heels clipped on the floorboards towards the dining room door. He stared at the door. He remained seated. Maybe the guest wouldn't notice. His stomach fluttered. Yes, she would notice him as he was wearing a blouse and had a long female hairstyle. And a dog collar. He hadn't been able to find any way to unlock it and Melissa didn't see it as urgent.

What would Melissa's guest be like? Would she laugh at seeing him in a skirt? Would she tell him he looked nice or pretty? His stomach whirled again at the thought of being told he was pretty and he felt a surge in his penis. That was weird.

The dining room door swung open. Melissa stood and strode towards it. Her head disappeared behind the door as the friends hugged. He heard air kisses. This guest was a good friend judging by the warmth of their greeting. Melissa stayed by the door.

"I'm sorry your journey was so bad tonight; that's London traffic for you," Melissa said. "You're here now. Come through."

Melissa stood back and her guest walked in. The heels were heavy on the floor, clip-clip. A blur of black leather coat and blond hair waved around her. Horror. His face dropped like a stone. It was Elizabeth. His wife.

He rocked back on his chair, his mouth gaped open like a fish as he gasped for air. Elizabeth, But how? Why?

Melissa read his mind. "Elizabeth and I are good friends from the London Businesswomen's Guild. As soon as you turned up here I called her. It seemed the right thing to do. Of course, I made sure you were properly prepared and dressed for her."

He was frozen in his chair. His escape plan had collapsed around him like cardboard walls in an earthquake.

Elizabeth sat opposite him. "We didn't know where you'd gone, Patty. Taking off like that, tricking poor young Jackie Swann. Tut tut." She turned to Melissa. "I'll take this naughty girl home after dinner. I have so many plans for her. I've only just begun."

Patrick looked from Elizabeth to a grinning Melissa. He was back to square one.

End of Part 1

Dear Reader,

I hope you enjoyed the first of the three-part series, 'Petticoated and Pretty'.

Please could you also spare a moment to share your thoughts on Petticoated and Pretty 1 by posting a quick review?

If you enjoy my forced feminisation stories, then why not subscribe to my blog at ***www.ladyalexuk.com*** *where I write about my true-life FLR with my pretty feminised husband Alice.*

You can also subscribe to my newsletter from my blog and receive occasional exclusive offers and stories.

Thank you so much for reading my stories,

Lady Alexa

xxx

Printed in Great Britain
by Amazon